Other books by Richard Kurti

*Monkey Wars*

# MALADAPTED

## RICHARD KURTI

WALKER
BOOKS

First published 2016 by Walker Books Ltd
87 Vauxhall Walk, London SE11 5HJ

2 4 6 8 10 9 7 5 3

Text © 2016 Richard Kurti
Cover illustration © 2016 Levente Szabó

This book has been typeset in Cambria

Printed and bound in Great Britain by Clays Ltd, St Ives plc

British Library Cataloguing in Publication Data:
a catalogue record for this book is
available from the British Library

ISBN 978-1-4063-4629-9

www.walker.co.uk

www.richardkurti.com

"Make Yourself at Your Peril."
Revelation, *Tenet 3*

# 1

"*1,107 DAYS WITHOUT A SINGLE DELAY,*" the Metro carriage announced with a smug ping. "*PROUD TO KEEP FOUNDATION CITY MOVING.*"

No-one took any notice of the soft electronic voice.

No-one except Cillian, who was disappointed.

Why hadn't he finished his assignment last night? He stared in frustration at the complex tangle of equations on his smartCell. No way would this be ready for the first lecture, and a Metro stuck in the tunnel would've bought him precious time.

Some hope.

He tapped his screen to enlarge the knot of numbers, when suddenly a heart icon pulsed briefly and a message scrolled across the display:

*Sorry to interrupt your browsing, but a girl in this carriage has Liked your profile.*

Cillian felt a flutter of excitement and glanced up. Everyone in the crowded carriage was silent, absorbed in the Ultranet: someone was playing a game, someone else was watching a movie, several were frantically catching up with emails. All of them were somewhere else…

His eyes darted from face to face, trying to work out who on this commuter train had pinged him, but no-one was giving anything away.

Cillian glanced at the man sitting next to him and cursed his luck. Why *now*? Why did he have to get pinged on the one morning a week he travelled Riverside with his father?

On the other hand, his dad wasn't really paying much attention. He was studying his touch-pad, enthralled by the latest twists in Foundation City's elections. Cillian had never understood why his father was so interested in politics – all the parties seemed pretty much the same, constantly trying to outdo each other's promises of lower taxes and tighter security.

Cillian looked back to his own screen and decided to go for it. He tapped the smartCell: *Tell me more.*

A profile opened. *Pixel-Girl, 19. Image Researcher. Likes clubbing, movies, gaming.* Her photograph was tantalizingly obscured.

*Would you like to send a Flirt?*

What could he say? Numbers were his thing, not words. He racked his brains…

*She'll be leaving at the next stop, Cillian.*

Think, think. He'd made a *DigiFlirt* profile after someone in his class circulated the hack codes, and had been tweaking it ever since. His total lack of success meant he hadn't really thought about what to do if someone actually showed an interest.

Cillian felt the Metro decelerate as it approached the station. In a panic he touched the *Flirt For Me* tab.

He had no idea what charming line the app came up with, but a few moments later: *Pixel-Girl has gone visible.*

Cillian tapped *Camera* and discreetly tilted his smart-Cell up. A live image of the gently rocking carriage played on the screen ... then a glowing heart superimposed above one of the passengers.

The girl looked up, caught his eye and gave a half-smile. Pixel-Girl was pretty, but she looked as new to this as he was.

As the Metro slid to a stop, the girl stood up and joined the shuffle towards the doors.

What now? He had about 3 seconds until she was gone.

Think. Think!

But Pixel-Girl was ahead of the game. As she jostled out, she let her smartCell swipe past his just long enough to send a DigiKiss, and then she was gone.

The Metro pulled away and Cillian opened the message: *You look cute when you're nervous!* followed by her email. Maybe she wasn't such a newbie after all.

Then just as he tapped to store her address, he caught his father's eye.

"What?" Cillian swiped his screen back to the equations. "I'm just finishing my assignment."

"Right." Paul nodded. "Nothing like Number Theory to put a smile on your face."

"I guess." Cillian frowned, pretending to be absorbed in his work. "This is really tricky stuff..."

"Does she know you're only 16?"

Cillian felt himself blush. "Dad, half the people on there are underage. Everyone does it."

Paul smiled. "You're the one who's going to have to think fast when she suggests going to a bar."

"Shouldn't you be getting ready for your stop?" Cillian said, trying to sink deeper into his seat.

"Don't worry. I'm gone." But just as Paul started to fold his touch-pad away, a strange shudder pulsed through the carriage.

Cillian looked up, immediately sensing the disruptive patterns of energy ricocheting around the carriage.

"What's wrong?" Paul recognized the eerie sense of deep calm that possessed his son; normally it was when he was focussed intently on something, but now there was fear in its undertow.

"I see it," Cillian whispered.

Paul braced himself, his fists tightened.

Another strange pulse. The smartCells and tablets in everyone's hands scrambled.

A flicker of chaos, then all the screens blacked out.

Dead.

"It's going to be OK." Paul touched his son's arm, trying to reassure him.

"No ... it's not." The sickly taste in Cillian's throat told him something terrible was coming.

Suddenly a dreadful screech, metal on metal, tore painfully at the air.

Violent hammering thundered through the floor, loud and urgent, like brakes desperately trying to lock in—

Trying and *failing*.

The carriage doors snapped open and hot air blasted in.

Reinforced walls of the tunnel flashed past.

Alarms wailed as systems collapsed.

The train lurched violently from the tracks and smashed into the tunnel ceiling—

Ploughing into solid concrete—

Blinding flashes seared through the carriage—

Clouds of burning sparks spewed from the ventilation grilles—

And people screamed in terror as they were engulfed by savage chaos.

# 2

Running the SkyWay was the perfect alibi.

Hundreds of metres above the road grid, rubbing shoulders with the glistening curtain walls of the Financial District, Tess couldn't be further from the Metro.

This jogging track was all about extremes. It was running-with-adrenaline, designed to feel exhilarating and dangerous. You crossed bridges suspended high over steel and glass canyons, then spiralled around the peaks of skyscrapers.

And now was the perfect time: after the hordes of futures traders and tech-hub entrepreneurs had scrambled to their desks, but before the leisure runners started clogging up the SkyWay. It meant Tess would easily be picked out by the host of CCTV cameras, exactly as she'd planned. Right now she looked like just another jogger training for the Snow Marathon.

A perfect alibi.

As she pounded the metal treads, her breath billowing

in the freezing winter air, Tess let her eyes wander across the vista. There was no denying that on the surface Foundation City was an impressive sight, and from up here you could actually see it evolving, reinventing itself with a restless energy, the skyline pushing higher every year.

*A beacon of fluid-finance.*

*A driver of cutting-edge technology.*

*Better, faster, freer, healthier.*

Everything about Foundation was aspirational ... but Tess had seen deeper. She knew that the high-gloss covered a profane ugliness that had to be exposed.

She glanced at the lines of cranes far away on the horizon, manically working at the City's margins, tearing down the old with ruthless efficiency. *That* was the truth. Foundation City was a steel and glass cancer, constantly consuming to keep itself alive, destroying anything that stood in its way.

If you really believed in The Faith, if you'd devoted your life to its principles, you couldn't just stand by and watch. It wasn't an option. You had to act.

And now she had.

As the running track passed the terrace of the Eastern Currency Pinnacle, Tess paused at a Workout Station and scanned her smartCell across the Fitness-Post, just to make sure the system knew she was here. The screen congratulated her on *Above average speed for a 17-year-old female* then immediately set her a harder target.

Typical Foundation. Nothing was ever good enough. Success and achievement were always marbled with discontent. That was how the City got its claws into you and drove you harder.

She leapt up and grabbed a steel crossbar to rattle off

30 pull-ups, hard and fast, relishing the little stab of pain with each one.

But at 23 she heard a distinctive mechanical clicking and craned her head around – a small group of Maintenance-Bots had appeared further along the track.

Originally the City authorities had closed the SkyWay when the ice storms hit, but as the winters became longer and more severe they'd had to think again, and the small army of strangely shaped Maintenance-Bots became a permanent feature. Now they spent their entire existence up here, roaming back and forth, diligently clearing snow and de-icing 24/7.

As she got closer, the Lookout-Bot sensed her footfall and swivelled its scanning head around. The bots were programmed to zip into the steel skeleton under the treads as soon as anyone approached, so Tess stopped dead still, trying to fool their pattern recognition software.

The Lookout hesitated, re-scanned with its infrared eyes, noted that the blob of heat was stationary, and turned away.

Tess crept closer ... closer ... until she could hear the gentle purr of the bots' servos, then suddenly she sprinted hard, hurtling straight for the machines.

The smaller ones scampered for the shadows, but the algorithms of the larger ones knew they wouldn't make it in time, and froze in panic.

"Too slow." Tess laughed as she ran past. "Way too slow."

They'd certainly have her in their database now.

As she ran through the steaming Glasshouse Gardens on the roof of the Central Bank, Tess checked her watch. Shouldn't she have heard something by now?

Her mind flashed back 8 hours, going over everything again: infiltrate the depot as part of a cleaning crew ... middle carriage, third row of seats ... unscrew the panel ... place the device on top of the cabling hub exactly as instructed.

Tess felt a small thrill of satisfaction – this was her first real chance to prove to Revelation that she was an operator who could work alone. She'd shown how tough she was in the squad that pulled off the arson attack on the Venture Capital Exchange. *Great job,* Blackwood had said. *Really great job.* And he wasn't one to lavish praise.

That was why he'd selected her for this. Blackwood could have chosen anyone, but he chose her, and now she would make him proud.

In a few moments Foundation City would get the message: it was a fool's paradise that showed no respect for the sacred.

And not everyone was impressed by its arrogant wealth.

# 3

A deafening screech of metal ripped the air—

And the Metro slammed into the train ahead with a violent jolt that tore passengers from their seats.

Cillian saw briefcases and smartCells hurtle through the carriage like flying shrapnel. In the explosion of chaos, his mind surged into overdrive ... and everything fell silent.

Suddenly he could hear *nothing*.

The terrified cries and twisting shriek of grinding metal *vanished* as if the air had been sucked out of the train, as if they were in a vacuum.

It made no sense.

*No sense.*

Cillian felt his heart beat once—

Then time itself ... slowed ... down.

He saw his father get plucked from his seat and tumble in slow motion through the carriage, colliding with other bodies in free fall, their limbs flailing.

He saw the carriage walls slowly concertina.

Panels bulged and blew inwards, scything through falling bodies.

Windows burst into showers of glass that sprayed gracefully across the collapsing space.

The metal handrail next to him quivered, then popped from its fixing to become a lethal spear. Cillian watched helplessly as a falling man tumbled towards it and was impaled through his stomach in agonizing slow motion, blood blossoming across his shirt.

Escape.

Cillian had to escape.

He felt energy surge through his body—

Galvanizing him—

Pushing him to survive.

He reached out to grab hold of the ceiling and was astonished to feel himself moving at normal speed. Somehow he was the *only* thing in this torment that wasn't unravelling in slow motion.

He launched himself across the carriage, reached out for his falling father and grasped his hand.

Paul looked up, fear and shock on his face. They hung there for a few precious moments, clinging on to each other as death lashed all around them. Then slowly Cillian hauled his father away from the rows of seats that had turned into metal jaws.

*Thump.*

Cillian felt his heart beat again – the train had collapsed in just a single impossibly stretched heartbeat. For a brief moment all the chaos around him focussed into in a coherent pattern—

*I see it.*

—and Cillian understood exactly how the clouds of

debris were moving, how the tumbling bodies were a perfect expression of momentum and gravity.

It all made sense...

Until the roof bulged and split as a steel girder sliced into the carriage—

Decapitating a falling girl in a green dress—

Slicing a fat man's torso in two, spilling blood in slow swirls of red mist.

Cillian tried to pull his father clear of the girder but it flashed too fast, cutting mercilessly into Paul's arm...

And he dropped away.

The air swelled with crackling heat as a tongue of flame licked through the carriage, then retreated.

With a gut-wrenching judder the Metro finally slammed to a halt.

Ringing pierced Cillian's brain, deafening him from the inside.

Then a chaotic wave of sound crashed in—

His mind jolted, and suddenly everything was happening at normal speed again.

Cillian could hear himself gasping for breath.

He could hear terrified sobs.

The creak of metal.

The delicate, thin sound of music spilling from headphones cast adrift in the crash.

Bodies were all around, bent at impossible angles.

What should he do?

Cillian swayed back and forth, paralysed with fear.

*What could he do?*

He heard a dull *thump*, then felt a sudden rush of heat. Fire.

It jolted him into action.

He clawed his way through the wreckage and onto

the track, glancing at the terrified faces of victims, staring into vacant eyes, until he found his father pinned between the wheels of the train, his body crushed by steel.

Feverish with adrenaline, Cillian tore at the metal, bending the axles with his bare hands, untangling the wreckage until he cradled his father in his arms.

A curtain of blood covered Paul's face and soaked his shirt. His skin was blackened with smoke, blood pumped from his arm—

But he was still breathing.

"It's all right..." Cillian sobbed, half crying, half gasping with relief. "It's all right."

There was still a flicker of life in his father.

A tiny flicker.

# 4

Tess checked the time again, then as if in answer to her prayers, the wail of a police siren rose up from the streets.

This was it. The blow had landed.

A second siren started, then a third. Tess stopped running and peered over the edge of the SkyWay; she saw the traffic signals far below snap to red, then one lane of the road pulsed blue, instructing everyone to clear. Moments later, emergency vehicles sped through, converging on the Floating Park district.

Tess felt a swell of pride. One well-placed device would gridlock the entire Metro system, and Revelation would be headline news again, forcing people to listen because that was the only way to make them understand.

But just as she turned to run on, a rhythmic thumping in the sky made her look up: helicopters. Not just one, but 4 ... 5 emergency choppers swarming over the river like insects. And not just the police, but medical SWAT teams carrying BioSpares.

Unease suddenly gnawed at Tess's guts. Why would they send those to trains stuck in tunnels?

She pulled her running gloves off with her teeth, fumbled for the smartCell in her pocket—

And froze.

Horrific images were feeding onto the Ultranet: smoke billowing from ventilation shafts, live-cams from rescue workers wading through debris, bodies being carried from a Metro station.

"No..." Tess swiped her screen. "This isn't it..." She flitted across the newsfeeds, but with each touch the news got worse: *Hundreds caught in Metro crash... Many feared dead... Fire engulfs commuter trains...*

Tess felt her knees give way and she crumpled onto the freezing running track.

"It can't be..."

But all the news sites said otherwise, bombarding her with images of carnage and chaos. Somehow the plan had gone wrong.

Irretrievably wrong.

Overwhelmed with nausea, she retched, painful, choking spasms making her gasp for breath—

*"Do you need medical assistance?"*

Tess looked up and saw a Maintenance-Bot peering down at her with dispassionate LED eyes. *"You seem to be in distress."* The voice was civil, devoid of emotion. *"Should I call for medical assistance?"*

"No ... no." With immense effort, Tess hauled herself to her feet.

*"Please stay where you are—"*

"No!"

The bot fell silent, as if sulking at the rebuke.

"It's... I'm all right," Tess said.

Hold it together, hold it together.

"It's just cramp. Really."

*"Cramp can be a serious condition,"* the ever-helpful bot went on. *"Please stay where you are so that I can call for assistance."*

"I'm OK. It's nothing." Tess turned and forced herself to run on.

Hold it together.

She raised a hand to wave her thanks to the bot, but didn't dare turn around in case its infrared eyes saw the tears streaming down her face.

# 5

"I've got you ... I've got you."

Cillian tried to hide his fear, but it felt like he was walking through hell. An acrid, burning hell.

He cradled his father tightly in his arms as he stumbled through the choking heat and smoke-filled darkness, forcing himself to block out all the death and carnage that filled the tunnel, to ignore the bodies and groans for help. If he was going to save his father, he had to stay focussed on the faint dot of light in the distance.

"You're going to be OK," Cillian whispered over and over, as he picked his way between the rails, hoping that somehow his words would keep Paul clinging to life. But he could feel his father's breathing getting shallower.

Keep walking ... one step at a time ... away from death, towards the light.

A news crew saw him first. Their dramatic images of black smoke billowing from the station entrance were being played in real time on the Ultranet, where millions watched in horror as their City came under attack again.

Momentarily the acrid smoke swirled aside to reveal a figure emerging from the darkness.

"Over there!"

For a few seconds everyone just stared, as the young man emerged into daylight, a bleeding victim draped in his arms, an image of hope amid destruction.

A miracle survivor.

The paramedic's urgent whistle broke the spell. "Resuscitation Team! Triage! Station entrance!"

As the smoke cleared, Cillian was overwhelmed. Rescue workers rushed towards him in a blur of movement. His father was plucked from his arms and put on a stretcher, medics bombarding his body with tubes and wires: oxygen, adrenaline, analgesics.

Cillian tried to follow, but other paramedics held him back.

"Relax." They lifted Cillian onto another stretcher. "We've got you."

Everything was confusion. He was blinded by a blizzard of flashing lights from the emergency vehicles and news crews. People were rushing everywhere, cutting equipment was going into the tunnel and body bags were coming the other way.

Cillian saw his father vanish into the mobile ER Unit and knew he had to be there with him. He swung his legs off the gurney—

"Don't move! Please!"

"I'm OK."

"You're in shock."

He tore off the tubes they were trying to fix to him and ran towards ER.

"WAIT!"

But Cillian wasn't stopping for anyone. He barged through the doors to the operating theatre—

Doctors huddled around Paul's body, issuing a stream of instructions in clipped tones; nurses were plugging his father into a bewildering array of monitors and life-support systems amid a cacophony of chirrups and beeps. A porter silently mopped up blood that was spilling onto the floor.

As he edged closer, Cillian saw his father's hand, the calm familiar hand that he'd known all his life – that he'd clutched as a young child – now sticky with blood, twitching as the nerves jangled.

He looked up at the monitors scrolling with Paul's vital signs—

*I see it.*

Instantly the pattern of frightening irregularities became apparent. He could see chaos stalking closer.

Someone grabbed Cillian and tried to pull him away. "You can't be in here."

"I'm not leaving."

"You need treatment—"

"*He's my father!* I'm not leaving!"

Through the tangle of drug lines he saw his father's eyelids flutter as he recognized Cillian's voice.

"Dad!"

With immense effort, Paul dragged open his eyes.

A doctor saw the connection flicker between them. "It's OK." The doctor nodded to Cillian. "You can stay." He pointed to a spot near the head of the gurney. "Talk to him. Don't let him... Just try to keep him here."

Cillian crouched next to his father and gently put his hands on his forehead. "I'm staying with you."

But when he glanced up, Cillian saw the silent language passing between the medics, the hesitations and anxious blinks.

He looked down at his father and saw his lips twisting as if he was fighting to say something.

"It's all right. Try to stay calm."

But his father seemed determined to get the words out, and his mouth battled against the drugs that were flooding his body.

*"Gilgamesh..."* It was barely audible, more of a gasp than a word.

Cillian didn't understand. The opiates must be scrambling his father's mind. "Don't worry. I'm here," he whispered, powerless to help.

But his father wasn't going to give up. Somehow he mustered the energy to feebly shake his head.

"Gilgamesh," he repeated, his eyes locked on his son, urging him to listen.

"Has he got BioSpares insurance?" The doctor's voice cut across the moment.

Cillian glanced up.

"Is he insured?" the doctor insisted. "His vital organs have haemorrhaged. He needs replacements. Urgently."

Cillian shook his head. They had nowhere near enough money for BioSpares.

He looked back to his father and saw him staring with such intensity, unable to muster the strength to say what he needed to say.

Cillian bent low so that their heads touched and he could feel his father's fragile breath on his face.

"I don't understand."

"Gil ... Gil..."

Suddenly Paul drew a deep breath. As he sucked in the air, his throat gurgled.

The data on the screens lurched, then started free-wheeling. The monitoring bleeps raced chaotically, fighting to keep up.

"Don't go!" Cillian pleaded. "Don't!"

Paul's eyes slid shut and he exhaled in a long sigh.

Cillian waited for his father to draw breath again, waited for the next beat of his heart.

But it never came.

The medical team drew back from the table.

Cillian watched the life drain from his father, saw pale blue tinge the pinkness of his lips.

And it was over.

A fist of pain thumped Cillian's chest.

Somewhere in the background he heard the doctor quietly say, "Time of death: 10.34. Notify the Digital-Executor."

Cillian remained absolutely still, his hands clasping his father's cooling face.

# 6

The catastrophic violence of the bomb had scrambled Tess's mind. She felt numb; all she wanted was to get away from the harrowing images flooding every Wall-Screen and electronic billboard across the City. She had to hide until she could get her head straight.

But where? The agreed rendezvous?

Too dangerous. The destruction would have blown all Blackwood's meticulous planning to pieces. Everything was different now and for all Tess knew Revelation had already been compromised, which meant she might be walking straight into a trap.

Where to go?

*Where?*

She looked out across the City, desperately hunting for ideas ... and saw the ring of cranes on the horizon. Maybe on Foundation's churning margins there was still hope.

\*\*\*

The shambolic rolling-estates couldn't have felt more different to Downtown. The noise and dust and confusion out here always left Tess reeling.

Everything was temporary. Pop-up shops and cafes sprouted and evaporated on a daily basis, buildings vanished and piling machines magically appeared overnight; all life here seemed transient and improvised.

A groaning *crack* echoed off the buildings as another huge slab of concrete crumpled to the street and kicked up a cloud of dust. Wherever Tess looked, cranes were tearing down old residential blocks, giant mechanical moles were boring gullies and bright hoardings announced new Metro lines and apartment complexes.

The noise and disruption was why it was so cheap to live out here, and why it drew so many young people trying to get a toehold in the City. Rents were low because there was no security. Landlords squeezed the last few weeks out of places before the bulldozers moved in, as yesterday's slums became tomorrow's Foundation City.

But while the half-complete infrastructure made life a gritty ordeal, it also meant it was a little easier to stay off-grid.

Sachin opened the door and stared at her in shock. "You can't be here!"

"I've nowhere else to go."

"Are you crazy?" He tried to shut the door, but Tess jammed it open with her foot. "Don't turn me away! Please."

He saw the anguish and confusion in her eyes. "Shit."

Reluctantly Sachin pulled her inside, checked no-one had seen and threw the bolts across.

"I didn't change the plan," Tess said.

"Well something went wrong."

"I swear! Every last detail was checked—"

"What difference does it make now?" He glared at her angrily.

"I just need somewhere to think." Tess walked down the hallway and entered the tiny lounge. A laptop was open on the table playing live images from the Metro tunnel. Rescue workers were cutting through the tangled wreckage and carrying out body bags.

"How many dead?" she whispered.

Sachin flipped the computer shut. "No point torturing yourself. You were doing your duty."

"How could that be duty?" she said bitterly.

"Following The Faith means just that, doesn't it?" Sachin lit up a smoke anxiously. "Following, not questioning."

"'While We Breathe, We Trust,'" Tess said in a hollow voice.

"Right. While We Breathe, We Trust." Sachin inhaled deeply. Tess could hear the doubt in his voice.

"Could I use the hole? Until it's safe again."

"I guess." Sachin stubbed out his smoke, then pushed the battered sofa aside, lifted a threadbare rug and removed 4 sections of floorboard to reveal a steel trapdoor. "Don't worry, I've cleaned it since you were last here." He gave a grim smile and swung the door open.

Carefully Tess clambered down the narrow steps into the darkness and dropped onto a mattress.

"The torch is by your foot."

Tess felt around until she found it and snapped the bulb on.

"You'd better have these as well." Sachin rummaged in his pocket and pulled out a small tin. He flipped the lid to reveal 2 red capsules.

"What are they?"

"You need to sleep."

Tess shook her head. "I need to find out what went wrong."

"You'll go crazy in the hole if you don't sleep. You know that. Just swallow them."

Tess looked at the capsules.

"Pray, then sleep. I'll try to make contact with Revelation." He wasn't going to take no for an answer, so reluctantly Tess did as she was told. Then Sachin closed the steel trapdoor and locked it.

Tess heard the sofa being dragged back into position above her and wondered how long she was going to be down here.

She looked around the tiny cell – no windows, no furniture, just the torch, the mattress and a small grille that let fresh air in through a pipe in the wall. Nothing had changed since the stem-cell engineer had been held here until his ransom was paid. Except that Tess had been on the other side of the trapdoor then, guarding him, making sure he was fed and washed.

Now *she* was in the hole.

Even so, for the first time since the explosion, Tess felt safe. Maybe if she never left the hole, she'd never have to face what she'd done. But in the darkness she could feel the rhythmic *thump, thump* of the pile drivers outside; soon this building would be consumed as well. She couldn't stay hidden for ever.

Slowly her limbs started to feel heavy as the sedatives kicked in. Tess curled up and closed her eyes.

# 7

Numb with shock, Cillian finally gave in to the para-medics' demands. Strangers' hands took control, placed him on a stretcher and wheeled him across the station concourse towards what looked like a medical imaging truck.

He didn't struggle.

He didn't question.

He didn't say anything at all. Now he was just another victim.

As he was wheeled past the growing line of body bags on the pavement, Cillian saw that the medics had given way to heavily armed Special Ops teams. That meant it was a terror attack rather than an accident. Not that it made any difference to the people he'd been sitting next to in the carriage.

Inside the truck, the scanner powered up and its deep hum blocked out the sounds of crisis and emergency.

Now all Cillian could feel was emptiness inside.

As the mechanical arm danced around him, he studied the nurses' faces. In the reflections on their glasses, he saw colourful real-time images from inside his own body unfolding on the display screens.

But the more they scanned, hunting for internal injuries, the more puzzled the nurses became. Cillian saw their glances flick anxiously across the screens as if they were struggling to make sense of the body-maps, then he heard someone pick up the phone and call for a doctor.

They'd obviously found something wrong. Deeply wrong; maybe some kind of brain injury. It was the only thing that could explain the terrifying strangeness of the crash: the violence unfolding in slow motion, his freakish ability to outmanoeuvre the carnage as if he'd somehow been ripped out of normal time, the inexplicable strength that had let him twist aside the steel chassis to free his father.

Cillian held up his hands and gazed at them as if they were something alien. An hour ago it had just been a normal Wednesday morning; he'd understood how the world worked. Now nothing made sense.

Not even his own father.

Gilgamesh. The word hung darkly in his head.

What did it mean?

Desperately hunting for a clue, Cillian's mind started speeding back over the life they'd shared: places they'd been to, things they'd talked about, books they'd read, movies they'd seen.

Gilgamesh ... Gilgamesh...

But his mind kept drawing blanks.

The word meant nothing to Cillian. Why had it meant

so much to his father that he'd used his dying breath to utter it?

"Do you know what's happened?" The nurse's abrupt voice cut across his thoughts. Before Cillian could answer, she shone a torch into his eyes, making him wince.

"Yes," he said, trying to turn aside.

The nurse studied his face intently. "You've been in an accident—"

"I know," he interrupted. "I know."

The nurse looked at him strangely, then whispered to her colleague, "He's still in shock."

Cillian glanced to his right and saw his reflection in yet another screen. He looked so relaxed, as if lying here was the most natural thing in the world.

Why was he so calm?

Why wasn't he in pieces, sobbing inconsolably?

What the hell was wrong with him?

# 8

For a few precious moments after she woke, Tess felt a deep sense of peace. Her eyes focussed on a tiny speckle of sunlight that had dodged through the ventilation grille, and she watched for a few moments as it fluttered on the wall.

Then with a jolt she remembered, and heaviness overwhelmed her again. From now on, her world would always be stained with a bloodshed that would never wash clean.

She heard the sofa scrape across the floor above, and braced herself. A few seconds later the trapdoor swung open and a dark shadow loomed over her.

"You OK?"

It took a few frightening seconds to recognize him.

"Blackwood?"

As the figure crouched down and stretched out a hand, light from the lounge spilled across his face. Blackwood was muscular, with a soft, neat beard. He looked young, but he had the certainty of someone much older, and his brown eyes exuded reassurance.

"Come on." His strong grip lifted her up into the room.

"What went wrong?" Tess demanded.

"You have to stay calm."

"Tell me! What went wrong?"

"Tess, you're angry and upset. I get that—"

"You have no idea what I'm feeling! Do you know how many people died today?"

But Blackwood wouldn't be drawn. "We're all so proud of what you've done—"

"How can you be proud of murder?" She couldn't hide the disgust in her voice. "*Tell me!*"

"The people who died today had no respect for what's sacred. You need to understand—"

"I understood what was *supposed* to happen," Tess cut across him. "The electromagnetic pulse was *supposed* to knock out the train's systems, gridlock the Metro, not kill and maim."

"Their fail-safes failed. That's not your fault, and it's not mine."

She stared at him, incredulous. "How can you be so calm? After what we just did?"

"We've done nothing wrong."

"*I* planted the bomb. *You* ordered it. *We* killed them."

"Listen to me. It was their own arrogance that killed those people."

"It was supposed to be a protest! Not murder."

"Their technology failed them when they needed it most. How much more proof do you need?"

Tess looked down to avoid the dark intensity of Blackwood's gaze.

"Maybe now Foundation City will start to realize how

misguided it is."

"Since when did we become executioners?"

"This is what courage looks like." Blackwood reached out and lifted her face. "The courage to make a stand. And you have nothing to worry about. There's no trace you were ever in that carriage – we've made sure of that. Revelation will protect you no matter what. You know that, don't you?"

Tess said nothing.

"Now pray with me."

"No."

"It'll help."

"It won't." Before she could stop herself, Tess felt her tears drip onto her hands.

"Don't ... please..." Blackwood put his arms around her and held her tightly. "Truth is never an easy path to follow. That's why we have The Faith."

"They were just innocent people," she whispered.

"They weren't. No-one we have ever targeted has been innocent. In its rush for progress, Foundation is more ruthless than we will ever be. We have principles, but Foundation has nothing, only greed and arrogance. The City needs to unravel because it's wrong, and it's Revelation's duty to be at the heart of that struggle. We are stormtroopers of The Faith." He held her hands in his, firm and reassuring. "Only the weak would stand by and do nothing. But you're not weak, Tess. You are one of the strongest we have."

"I don't feel strong."

"Without The Faith, what we did was senseless murder. But *with* it, we are fighting a just cause."

Her eyes flicked over his face. He was offering her a lifeline.

"The Creator Made Man from Love," Blackwood urged. "But the only thing Foundation City loves is wealth. And ambition. And technology. And insatiable change. People have lost sight of what really matters. That's why we're fighting."

And finally, Tess glimpsed a way that her blood-soaked future could make sense.

"Even though the carnage wasn't intended, I really believe it was the Creator's will," Blackwood said.

"How can we ever know for sure?"

"Because the horror of the bomb has exposed a much darker horror." He reached into his jacket, took out a smartCell and swiped open a photograph.

Tess looked at the picture of a teenage boy carrying his dying father out of the swirling black smoke.

"Who is he?"

"Not who," Blackwood warned. "But *what*."

# 9

Cillian didn't know how long he'd been lying in the Trauma Ward; it seemed like hours since they'd transferred him to the Liberty Hospital, but he couldn't be sure.

They'd isolated him in a high-dependency cubicle and plugged him into all manner of BioMonitors, making it impossible for him to get up.

On the bedside table one of the nurses had laid out the things they'd found in his pockets. He reached for his smartCell and turned it on. Messages scrolled across the screen, from concerned friends, colleagues of his father and there were even some from pushy journalists trying their luck.

Cillian swiped the screen clear; he couldn't face dealing with anyone yet. But just as he was about to toss the smartCell back, he noticed the social media apps blinking furiously. He touched the icons and was astonished to see streams of new messages: propositions from

*DigiFlirt, Friend Requests, Buddy-Ups* and *Likes,* hundreds of taps from complete strangers. As he glanced through the feeds, he realized they were all chattering about TV images of him emerging from the burning Metro station. A few had even made snappy compilations to licks of music.

While his father was dying, Cillian had been going viral on the Ultranet.

Nauseated at being some kind of ghoulish celebrity-of-the-moment, Cillian blocked all the social apps. He needed silence to think, to get his bearings.

The door clicked open and a tall medic with a shiny face entered; Cillian recognized him as the doctor who had tried to save his father.

"How are you doing now?"

He couldn't even begin to answer a question like that.

"I'm Dr Lomas." Gently he sat down next to the bed. "We tried everything, but your father's injuries—"

"He was a doctor too," Cillian said bitterly.

"I didn't know that."

"He spent his life helping people, but when he needed it, you let him die."

"I'm sorry. But everyone in that carriage..." Lomas's words tailed off awkwardly.

"Why are you keeping me here?" Cillian glanced at the monitors and could immediately see there were no irregularities in the patterns of the data. "Unless you've found something wrong?"

Lomas was taken aback by his directness. "We just need to make sure. After what you've been through, you're lucky to be alive."

*"Lucky?"*

"I'm sorry. I didn't mean..."

Cillian looked at Lomas intently, trying to understand what he was really thinking. Something didn't seem right about the doctor's sympathy.

"Do you remember much about what happened?" Lomas asked. "It just seems impossible for anyone to have walked out of that unscathed."

So that was it. They knew something strange had played out in the carriage, but they didn't know what.

"Why do you need to know?" Cillian asked warily. "Isn't it enough that I'm alive?"

"Of course. It's just..." Lomas stood up, leant across and started scrolling through different scans on the monitors. "A few cuts and bruises, a bit of smoke inhalation." He stared at the images. "It's incredible."

Cillian tried to read the doctor's face; he could see how baffled he was, how hungry for answers. Part of him was screaming to open up and tell someone about the inexplicable strangeness of the crash, but another part was warning him that maybe he shouldn't trust this stranger.

They looked at each other in silence for a few moments, before Lomas realized he wasn't going to get any more. "When you're ready, you'll need to see the hospital clerk. There are some formalities." He smiled uneasily and turned to go.

"When can I see my father's body?"

"I'm afraid ... that's not going to be possible. It was another terror attack. Revelation ramping up their tactics." Lomas rocked uneasily from one foot to the other. "So everything is evidence. Including the bodies. Sorry." And with that, he hurried out into the corridor.

Cillian watched the door as it slowly clicked shut, leaving him alone again.

Alone and baffled.

He was being bombarded with ragged bits of information that refused to fall into a pattern. He closed his eyes, desperate to think, to concentrate so that he could understand—

A sudden barrage of flashes interrupted his thoughts. Cillian gave a sharp tug at the tubes and wires tying him down, pulling them all off his body, and walked over to the window.

There was a scrum of photographers and news crews on the hospital forecourt, teeming around the City Mayor, who appeared to be giving a press conference. It was impossible to hear what he was saying through the sealed windows, so Cillian flicked on the WallScreen.

*"...marks a terrible escalation in the tactics of the extremists. They hide behind their Faith, but the truth is they are violent criminals, attacking the values we hold dear: innovation and technology, freedom and profit; a modern, democratic city where people can realize their dreams, fulfil their potential, build a better future. I promise you, those who seek to destroy our values will not succeed."*

Cillian remembered how his father had always thought that beneath the bonhomie, the Mayor was ruthlessly ambitious. He wouldn't have been impressed by this attempt to spin tragedy into political advantage.

*"The terrorists who have attacked Foundation City will be hunted down. There will be no hiding place for—"*

"What do you think you're doing?" An intensive care nurse ran into the room, ushering Cillian back towards the bed. "You can't just unplug yourself. We thought you'd had a heart attack."

Immediately she started resetting the monitors and

trying to reattach Cillian, but he pulled away.

"I want to go home now."

"You'll have to talk to the doctors—"

"No. I don't have to talk to anyone. I don't belong here."

# 10

Gabrielle sat in silence, her fingers flicking between the news feeds on her tablet, searching for an unexpected announcement that somehow Paul had survived. But all she found was one blood-soaked image after another.

And amid the carnage one particular image kept recurring: Cillian emerging from the smoke, Paul draped in his arms as he drew his final breaths.

She put the tablet down and cradled her head in her hands. Memories of Paul tumbled through her mind: his wry laugh, his logical mind, the determination in his eyes that tried to hide his sadness. More than anything, she remembered his courage; he knew they were stepping outside conventional morality, but he'd never faltered.

Now all his talents had been wiped out in an instant, defeated by ignorance, destroyed by people who refused to accept the true power of science.

It was a bitter irony that this was exactly why

Gabrielle had started P8 all those years ago: to fight the dreadful fragility of life.

She paced over to the gallery rail and gazed down into the cavernous open-plan void, criss-crossed with glass and steel walkways. P8's headquarters had been designed to inspire. The space was flooded with light, all the faint-hearted scepticism of the world kept out by a wall of secrecy. In this protected space, people could think freely, quietly push the boundaries of understanding...

And they did.

Now the results were out there, walking in the world.

She picked up her tablet and enlarged the still of Cillian holding Paul's maimed body. Without knowing why, people had been captivated by this raw depiction of survival. Even though they didn't know the truth, on some level they seemed to sense it. They were drawn to it *instinctively*.

Instincts.

If there was one thing Gabrielle's research at P8 had taught her, it was that primal instincts were one of the most powerful forces in nature.

She tapped the image to reveal its stats: half-a-million shares already. That was vindication enough. Determination tightened in Gabrielle's guts; she must not waver.

To be intimidated by terrorism would be to betray Paul's memory. She hadn't flinched in the past; she would not flinch now.

She tapped *Messaging* and summoned her team.

# 11

The 3 of them walked briskly under the glass dome of the roof solarium, their sneakers squeaking on the rubberized floor.

"We know it's Revelation," Cole said, diligently handing Gabrielle a set of pictures showing various electronic billboards across the City. "These were all taken in the last hour."

Gabrielle flicked through the printouts. Each one showed a display that had been hacked, its shimmering advert replaced by the ominous warning: *How dare you sport thus with life?*

"It shows how frightened they're getting," Gabrielle said pensively.

"You know, I wouldn't be so sure it *is* Revelation," Paige objected. "It's a huge change in tactics for them. Kidnappings and cyber-attacks are more their style."

"But they're being pushed into a corner." Gabrielle handed the pictures back. "Deep down, Revelation knows it's only a matter of time before the laws are relaxed. And when we finally come out and publish, people will be astonished at what we've achieved."

"But what if public opinion is actually against us?" Paige said.

"Knowledge drives this City. Unless Foundation legitimizes what we're doing, there'll be a brain drain. And that's how city states die."

"They also die through anarchy and terror," Paige said anxiously. "They implode."

"We need to hold our nerve," Gabrielle said calmly. "In the short term, the less people listen to Revelation, the louder it will scream and the more dangerous it'll become. It's why fanatics always turn to violence in the end."

"Well they certainly know how to tap into money," Paige said. "To knock out the Metro with a pulse-bomb, that takes some doing."

"Money and destruction always find each other." Gabrielle gazed through the glass wall of the dome, looking out across the skyline. "It's people who want to create things that struggle."

"All I'm saying is they won't be easily stopped."

"I know." Gabrielle nodded. "You're right. But nothing we do here is easy."

"On a more practical note," Cole was anxious to ease the tension between the 2 women, "it means Cillian's at risk. Revelation will have seen his picture. They'll be putting two and two together. It'll make him a target now. We should help him."

"Not necessarily," Gabrielle said, turning the problem over in her mind.

"We can't protect him unless we bring him in."

"Let's think it through. The whole point is to leave them out there, right? To see how they behave, how they integrate."

"Normally, yes. But—"

"So if we bring Cillian in, we risk wasting his entire Line."

"Surely we'd be *saving* the Line?" Paige wasn't going to back down. "We owe it to him to keep him safe."

"No-one wanted things to turn out like this. But now it's happened, we have an incredible opportunity."

"You'd seriously risk sacrificing him?"

"No-one's sacrificing anyone." Gabrielle was adamant. "And that kind of emotive language doesn't help."

Paige flipped her sunglasses down, covering her eyes.

"We have to be smart, logical," Gabrielle said. "We can play this to our advantage. Cole, you see what I'm saying?"

"Yes, but … you have to admit, without his father, Cillian's vulnerable."

"And vulnerable is interesting. I'm fascinated to see what he does now, with no protection."

Cole nodded. "I get that."

"Paige?" Gabrielle looked at her searchingly. "We all need to be behind this."

Paige hesitated; she seemed reluctant to get into a full-scale confrontation. "Sure." She nodded tersely.

"Which means our immediate concern is dealing with loose ends. Paul wouldn't have had a chance to tidy things up. He may have left us exposed."

"I'll brief security," Cole said, turning to go. "They can start covering our tracks."

"Make sure they're thorough," Gabrielle warned. "You know how I hate carelessness. For want of a nail, and all that."

# 12

The cold air slammed into Cillian as he left the stifling, overheated hospital. He dug his hands into his pockets and started to walk.

But where to go?

No way could he face the empty apartment, not just yet; it was still too raw. He'd have to take refuge in the university instead.

Because he'd won a Fast-Track scholarship 3 years early, he wasn't expected to live in like all the other students. Instead the university had given him a dedicated study-pod, a room where he could bunker down and lose himself in numbers whenever he wanted. Right now that felt like the safest place in the world, a cocoon of solitude.

The flurry of winter in the city drifted past. Everywhere he looked, Cillian's mind instinctively picked out evolving patterns and translated them into numbers: how the smoke rose from street stalls roasting chestnuts, the ebb and flow of people on the crowded pavement, the complex rhythms of steam billowing from the Maintenance-Bots that kept the sidewalks clear of ice.

For as long as he could remember, Cillian had been able to see the mathematics behind the world the way other people saw colours. His mind could effortlessly wrap itself around the most abstract patterns; and yet despite all that, he was completely baffled as to why his life had just unravelled so catastrophically.

It left him feeling strangely alienated, as if all along, the streets and buildings of Foundation City had been nothing more than a painted backcloth that had torn under his fingers like a bit of stage scenery. Right now the only solid things in his life were the granite paving slabs under his feet, and he felt a primal urge to keep walking on them.

As he turned into Lepanto Plaza, Cillian saw the ice rinks swirling with young children speeding carelessly in circles, their nervous mothers struggling to keep up.

Memories flooded back of his father bringing him here on Saturday mornings. He'd always imagined the skating rinks would become a kind of family tradition, and somewhere in his mind were fanciful images of him taking his own kids on the ice while Paul filmed it all.

Now the mental sketches of what might have been had to be wiped.

Suddenly Cillian felt a deep longing for human contact. He took out his smartCell, then remembered that he'd blocked all his social apps. Edging into the busiest part of the crowd, he stopped dead and let the throng of people flow around him, trying to feed off their energy: office workers hurrying back from lunch, students laughing and drinking coffee as they cycled past, tourists on frantic schedules.

But now that he looked closely, Cillian realized that for all the crowds and bustle, no-one was *really* here. One way or another they were all plugged into the Ultranet, living somewhere else, laughing with someone else.

All people did *here* was glance at each other.

Glance and move on.

Had it always been like this? Why had it never bothered him before?

His sense of unease deepened when he got back to university.

The familiarity of these surroundings should have been comforting, but as he stood by the doors leading to the atrium, Cillian was filled with dread. He had always loved this space with its polished maple floors, its sofas and media stations and huddles of students. But now all he saw were people bristling with attitude and over-trimmed beards. Suddenly the students logged into their Contact-Webs seemed like complete strangers, and Cillian wondered how he'd ever had anything to say to them.

He had to get away from all this, back to the security of his pod.

Head down, he hurried across the atrium—

"Cillian!"

"Hey! Are you OK?"

"They said you were in the hospital."

"We were worried—"

"We saw the pictures—"

"Is your dad—?"

He ignored everyone, pushed through the far doors and escaped into the elevator.

# 13

The door swung open and Cillian's study-pod immediately welcomed him. Lights faded up, images started scrolling across digital picture frames, a new track he'd found online a few days ago pulsed from hidden speakers.

As diary reminders flashed on the WallScreen, the female RoomVoice calmly updated him. *"Hi Cillian everyone's been trying to get hold of you. Would you like me to run through the messages?"*

He glanced at the WallScreen. "It doesn't matter now."

The ever-helpful operating system was undeterred. *"I can prioritize the list—"*

"Just forget everything."

*"But Cillian, some of these really need to be dealt with."*

"Do you know what death is?" he asked the room.

A moment of puzzled silence.

"My father's dead. He was killed this morning."

No response. It was as if the programmers hadn't wanted to consider this particular scenario.

"There was a crash on the Metro. A bomb attack."

*"The City's Metro has an impeccable safety record—"*

"Not today! Not today..."

A pause.

*"Would you like me to find the name of a grief counsellor?"*

"That's it? That's the best you can come up with?" Cillian challenged the room. "Do you even understand what I'm talking about?"

The RoomVoice maintained a sulky silence, then decided it was safer to switch tack. *"I've downloaded copies of the lectures you missed if you want to catch up."*

Had his room always been this dumb?

It was unnerving. Cillian had loved setting this space up to fit him like a glove, everything tailored to his own personal needs and taste. Yet now it felt as if he didn't belong here, as if this was a stranger's room.

Numbers. He had to escape into his studies – they were his bedrock.

He touched the large tablet on his desk and complex number patterns appeared on the screens, exactly as he'd left them yesterday. He rested his fingers on the algebraic keypads, cleared his mind and slipped into the vast, mysterious landscape of Number Theory. His fingers tapped out a complex dance that only he understood, paused momentarily, then raced on. Every now and then he flicked his thumb and the workings transferred to the WallScreen, decorating his room with formulae that probed and tried and failed, then tried again.

Suddenly he was distracted by a speck of dirt on the screen. He stretched out to clean it, and as his focus shifted he caught sight of himself reflected in the glossy surface.

He froze.

"What the hell am I doing?" Cillian stared at his

reflection, appalled at his calm expression. "Shit!" He kicked the chair back as he recoiled from the desk. "What's wrong with me?"

He stood in bewildered silence. His father had just been murdered, and here he was finishing his assignment. Cillian turned and gazed into the mirror, studying his own inscrutable eyes. *"What is wrong with me?"*

He shook himself to his senses, picked up the chair, sat back at the desk, swiped all the number screens away and typed a single word into the search engine: *Gilgamesh*.

*A Mesopotamian king from 3000 BC.*

*A jazz fusion band.*

*The hero of an epic poem.*

*A Michelin-starred restaurant.*

*A now-defunct baseball team.*

*A mythical city in a fantasy game.*

*A teaching hospital in the Provinces.*

Cillian's eyes held on the last line. He clicked the link. Gilgamesh: a huge hospital-hub, 1,200 kilometres from Foundation City, serving vast swathes of the sparsely populated Provinces.

He escalated the search, linking it to his father's name … and came across a single entry: 20 years ago, Paul had trained at Gilgamesh.

It didn't make sense. His father had never mentioned the hospital, not once, and yet it was so important that his dying words to his only child weren't "I love you", but "Gilgamesh".

Cillian couldn't see the pattern.

Nothing fell into place.

There was only jagged chaos. And that was the one thing he couldn't handle.

# 14

Covert meetings were always tricky. The veiled instructions meant you could never be sure you were waiting in exactly the right place.

Dr Lomas checked his watch. He'd been standing under the silver canopy of the East Mall for 15 minutes and still there was no sign of his handler. Though he could certainly understand why he'd be running late – it had been a busy day for Revelation. As he'd made his way over here, Lomas had seen its cryptic messages pinging onto hacked advertising hoardings all across the City.

*I gazed on my victim, and my heart swelled with exultation.* That had caused quite a stir on the Overhead, with indignant drivers stopping to vent their anger.

*I too can create desolation; my enemy is not invulnerable* had appeared like a rash over the ads on the Metro, taunting 20 million law-abiding commuters.

Even as Lomas had been waiting at the mall, he'd seen *I will work at your destruction, nor finish until I desolate your heart* hijack the movie preview billboards. He'd watched as furious shoppers demanded the insulting screens be turned off, but none of the managers seemed to know how the displays worked. As a temporary measure they'd draped tarpaulins over the screens, plunging the *Frankenstein* quote back into darkness.

Revelation could be difficult to deal with, but Lomas did admire its instinctive feel for drama. It had taken an old Gothic horror story, long forgotten because of its anti-science agenda, and made it a call to arms, using it to show the dangers of scientific research and to prophesy the Fall of Man. Revelation's violent attacks were starting to change the way people thought about The Faith; what for decades had just been a hollowed-out and impotent religion was turning into a radical philosophy for change.

As a young man Lomas had been scathing about religion and its medieval mindset. But 20 years working in hospitals had made him think again. Too many times he'd seen medical advances keep people alive long after they'd given up the will to really live. In the obsession to keep bodies functioning, the soul had somehow been forgotten.

Suddenly his smartCell chirruped. It was from Blackwood: *In the shadow of the Cathedral.*

The doctor cursed under his breath. It had been a long day at the hospital and the last thing he needed was a change of plan, especially with so many police now flooding the transport system. But as he headed back towards the station to catch a shuttle to the Cathedral District, his smartCell chirruped again: *No.*

So Blackwood was already here, watching him.

The doctor's eyes darted across the scene: crowds of people defying the security warnings by trying to carry on as normal, drinking in late-night cafes, queuing for last-minute theatre tickets, watching buskers juggling burning swords. In the square opposite, blazing spotlights illuminated an ice sculpting competition that was drawing in crowds of people, who clustered around huge frozen blocks, mesmerized as shapes emerged under the hands of chainsaw-wielding artists: a giant boot, a peacock, Death and his scythe...

A smile broke across Lomas's face as he realized that one of the half-formed ice sculptures was a dome: the Cathedral of Veneration.

# 15

As he jostled through the crowds Lomas understood why Revelation had chosen this spot. People's jangled nerves were making them hyper-vigilant for any behaviour that looked suspicious, but here all eyes were on the ice sculptures, and the buzz of chainsaws made eavesdropping impossible.

He made his way around a slightly disturbing Leda and the Swan, and into the shadow of the ice cathedral, where he recognized Blackwood.

"Must've been a stressful day at the hospital. I appreciate you coming," Blackwood said as he handed Lomas a takeaway coffee. "Skinny latte, 1 sugar, right?"

"Thanks." Lomas was touched by the gesture.

Blackwood led him deeper into the throng. "So, did you talk to Cillian?"

"He's shocked and confused," the doctor said as he sipped the coffee. "But I don't think he suspects anything."

"He's too intelligent *not* to suspect."

"Nothing he said made me worry."

Blackwood smiled obliquely. "Maybe he just doesn't trust you."

Lomas was unsure how to react to that.

"What about his wounds?"

"There were none."

"Are you sure?"

"I checked the scans myself. All the other victims in his carriage suffered catastrophic injuries, massive internal haemorrhaging, fourth-degree burns, but Cillian ... barely a scratch on him."

Blackwood stopped walking and locked his thoughtful gaze on Lomas. "Is there any way it could have been luck?"

All the bodies that had been extracted from the Metro flashed through the doctor's mind, a dreadful catalogue of trauma. "No ... it was beyond luck."

"Then we really are at war," Blackwood whispered. For an unnerving moment, the muscles in his face tightened, tingeing his soft features with a hard ugliness.

Lomas suddenly had a desperate urge to get away. "Look, if I hear any more, I'll contact you, OK?"

But as he turned to go, Blackwood gripped his arm. "Give me his details."

"Sure." The doctor pulled up the file and transferred the data in a DigiKiss. "You really think he could be one of them?"

"Let's see..." Blackwood opened an app on his smart-Cell which swallowed Cillian's identity number, then started pulling up streams of data. "Changed school every few terms ... finally settled at an academy for gifted students ... university scholarship at 15 ... no hospital records ... no illness of any kind ... he's certainly not normal."

"How many do you think are out there?"

"That … is the multi-billion-dollar question."

"So Cillian might be the only one?"

Suddenly Blackwood gave a brisk smile. "You've done really well. If only everyone was as diligent. But he's not your responsibility now."

Lomas felt queasy in his guts. "He's still a kid. He's hardly dangerous."

Blackwood studied the doctor's face. "You believe in the Tenets of Faith?"

"Of course."

"Then put your trust in the Creator who made us. Never doubt that you've done the right thing here. Doubt is Weakness."

They heard a nearby crowd cheer as one of the ice sculptors completed a brilliant flourish.

"I think we've talked enough, under the circumstances. Good night, Dr Lomas."

And that was it. No more discussion. Blackwood turned and disappeared into the crowd.

# 16

The lobby of the Residential Spire always seemed so welcoming, especially in the bright morning sunlight. Maybe it was the smell of jasmine polish they used on the marble floor, or maybe it was just the sheer familiarity of the place, but even though his father was gone, Cillian still felt the comforting security of home.

Until he saw Hailey sitting on one of the leather sofas.

For as long as Cillian could remember, his father had worked at a Walk-In clinic in the Western Financial Quarter. Walk-Ins gave quick fixes to busy traders who were eager to get back to their desks, and most doctors just passed through, using the extra shifts to clear med-school debts. Paul was the only one who stayed for a long time. He seemed to like the fleeting nature of the friend-ships, almost as if he didn't want anyone to get too close. But the person he'd always been most wary of was the Practice Manager. "Hailey's damaged," he used to say. "And damaged people are always dangerous."

"I'm so sorry." As she crossed the lobby Hailey opened her arms to hug him, but instinctively Cillian bridled.

Hailey smiled uneasily, trying to cover the awkwardness of the moment. "Is there anything I can do to help?"

"No... Not really." He studied her. Right now she seemed pleasant enough; maybe she really was upset.

"Everyone at the clinic is so shocked."

"I know."

"How are you coping?"

Cillian shrugged.

"What about money? I mean, can you—"

"The lawyer's dealing with everything."

"Good. That's good."

But Cillian sensed there was something else on her mind.

"And the university counsellors are looking after you?"

"Something like that."

"Your father would want you to keep your studies going. It meant a lot to him."

"I know."

"So ... call me if there's anything you need."

Cillian nodded, but Hailey was the very last person he would ever turn to for help. No matter what she said, deep down he sensed a terrible coldness to this woman. Then as he turned towards the elevators—

"Can I come up for a minute?"

Cillian looked at her warily. "Why?"

"There's just ... it's a work thing."

"It's not really a good time."

"I need to see if your father had any patient records at home."

"Records? What are you talking about?"

"Some of the doctors catch up on paperwork outside clinic hours. I know Paul used to. And I just need the files back."

Cillian stared at her in disbelief.

"You understand, don't you?"

"No. I don't."

"It's a security issue," Hailey said, her jaw tightening slightly.

"He's in the morgue!" Cillian exclaimed. "They won't even let me see him, and you're worried about files?"

"There's no need to be like that."

"Like what? Upset?"

"I've got a business to run."

"Can you even hear yourself?"

"I thought you'd be old enough to understand."

"Just stay away from me! Stay away."

Cillian hurried for the elevators; mercifully one was already waiting, so he didn't have to spend a moment longer in her presence.

# 17

Right now Cillian didn't want *anyone* in the apartment, especially people he couldn't trust, and Hailey's sudden and unexpected appearance had put her firmly on that list. If he was going to make sense of his father's dying moments, he needed time to search and space to think.

As the elevator silently marked off floors, Cillian took the glowing encryption-tab from his pocket and studied it. The lawyer had been understandably reluctant to hand it over. "We normally advise the next of kin to let us tidy up the Digital Legacy first," Mr Pilgrim (LLB) had said.

What he really meant was sanitize.

With more and more people leaving WholeLife Archives behind, warts and all, lawyers right across the City were having a field day protecting dead clients from incriminating themselves. But it was the warts that Cillian was interested in. He didn't want an airbrushed version of his father; he wanted the truth.

There was a gentle ping as the elevator doors opened.

Cillian walked down the corridor with its impossibly shiny floor and took out the apartment keys. But as he arrived at the front door he hesitated. The handle was already pulsing blue. *Unlocked.*

Immediately his mind flashed back 24 hours, scanning through meticulously stored memories of leaving the apartment with his father. He replayed the sequence from different angles: *definitely* locked. Paul never took shortcuts with security, and even though they were late, he'd insisted on locking up and setting the alarms before they ran for the Metro.

A noise from behind the door jolted Cillian's senses. He put his ear to the polished hardwood and listened.

Footsteps.

Someone was *inside.*

Back away; call the police. He knew what he *should* do … but if he put all his trust in the authorities, would he ever find out what was really going on?

Silently he pushed the door open and saw a strange electronic box clamped over the Main Control Unit, LEDs scrolling, overriding the apartment systems.

He edged forwards, senses bristling.

A light was on in the lounge, and a shadow was moving. Cillian peered through the crack in the door and saw a figure hunched over his father's desk, methodically searching through all the drawers. He had a black baseball cap pulled low, gloves, sneakers, and CyberSpecs recording everything he looked at.

"What the hell are you doing?" Cillian exclaimed.

The intruder spun around and reached into his jacket.

"NO!" Anger electrified Cillian's body like a force possessing him, and he leapt across the room—

Impossibly fast—

His hands reached out, clamped around the intruder's head and slammed it into the wall.

Air grunted from the stranger's lungs. "No..."

But it was beyond Cillian's control. His grip tightened, fingers pressing furiously on the man's skull.

The intruder thrashed desperately, arms flailing. He managed to grab a steel cosh from his pocket and bring it cracking down across the side of Cillian's head.

The pain barely registered, the adrenaline rush was too strong.

THUNK! The cosh smacked into his head again and a crimson wash trickled down Cillian's face.

The smell of his own blood ramped up his rage. He grabbed the intruder's fist and crushed it in his hand, harder and harder until he heard a sickening *crack*. The intruder screamed in agony and dropped the cosh.

Cillian loomed over the man, who just stared at his broken fingers in disbelief.

*"Who are you?"* Cillian demanded.

An agonized grunt was all he got back.

"Tell me!" Pulsing with anger, he picked up the intruder and hurled him against the couch, sending the CyberSpecs skittering across the floor.

Cillian stalked menacingly after him, stunned at the overwhelming power in his veins. It was as if he was in someone else's body. "What do you want with me?"

He saw terror in the man's eyes.

*"What do you want?!"* Cillian was firing with too much energy and the intruder knew it. Scrambling for his life, he lunged for the hallway and bolted through the front door.

Cillian paused, drew breath. He felt no fear; this was a hunt now. He strode after the intruder, legs powering across the distance, senses alert to everything, and heard the click of fire doors closing up ahead.

Easy.

He sprinted down the corridor in pursuit and smashed open the doors into an emergency stairwell.

Stop.

Listen.

Feet on concrete – running upstairs.

No escape up there.

His prey was cornered.

Cillian pounded up the steps, 3 at a time, abandoning himself to the thrill of the hunt. He kicked open the final set of doors—

And was suddenly overwhelmed with light.

He was on the Solar Deck, where clusters of mirrors focussed sunlight onto massive arrays of panels to power the apartment building.

Cillian went absolutely still, tuning in to his surroundings, trying to sense his enemy.

At street level the fog was still clearing, but up here the light was hard and brilliant, making the solar panels creak.

Cillian stalked further out onto the deck. The only escape was back through the fire doors. Sooner or later his victim would have to make a break for it.

The quiet crunch of gravel.

Cillian froze.

*Crunch.* Over to the right – the intruder was trying to hide.

Move further right.

Outflank him.

Then with a lurch of disappointment, Cillian realized his mistake. He saw a TechBridge, a lattice of steel girders wound with power cables linking this Spire to the next one – *another* way out.

Suddenly feet scrambled on the roof shingle as the intruder darted for the bridge. Cillian chased after him, dodging between the solar panels—

Closing in fast—

Trying to head him off—

He *would* get him—

Without warning a bolt of searing heat slammed into Cillian.

He snapped his eyes shut, shielding his face with his hands, but the light was too intense and he dropped to his knees, twisting his head away, and crawled blind, hands groping, until he was out of the blistering beam of heat. He looked back. The intruder had spun one of the parabolic mirrors around, turning light into a weapon.

Cillian scrambled to the left, away from the scorching beam, but it was too late. He saw his enemy climb along the last few metres of the TechBridge and vanish into the building opposite.

Furious with himself, Cillian lashed out, punching the nearest mirror, which shattered under his fist.

# 18

Tess stepped off the tram at Cotton Wharf and shivered.

Nothing had changed. Stylish apartments converted from 19th-century warehouses still lined the dock; massive loading cranes, remnants of a grand industrial past now turned into street furniture, were still twinkling with winter lights.

And yet everything had changed. 2 days ago Tess had walked away from here as an agitator, a dissident. Now she was returning as a killer.

The pulse-bomb had blown away all her fuzzy thinking. As the smoke of shock cleared, she understood that her life would only make sense if she accepted that she was now a stormtrooper for The Faith until the day she died.

She walked briskly towards an old tea warehouse that had been turned into a private college: *Institute for Cultural Studies* was carved proudly above the huge steel doors. As she brushed past wealthy traders hurrying in the opposite direction on their way to work, Tess couldn't help feeling that familiar twinge of resentment. Unlike most of these people who lived in Cotton Wharf, she had *known* poverty: what it smelled like, how it cut into your soul.

When Tess had arrived in Foundation as an orphan and a refugee, she had been greeted with hostile indifference by a city that saw her as nothing but a burden.

*"Foundation City helps those who help themselves,"* was the proud civic boast.

But if you couldn't...

She remembered the series of Placement Homes with painful vividness: the humiliating catalogue of rejection, the adults who never had time, the tired clothes and crumpled shoes that were constant reminders of your worthlessness.

Until the moment when Blackwood had appeared from nowhere, like a miracle, and given her a world that wasn't tenuous. He placed her in a school run by The Faith, where people listened, where she woke up to the same faces that were there the previous night; where she learned to have hope again.

That complete strangers would reach out and offer salvation had filled the 9-year-old Tess with such burning loyalty, she'd dedicated her life to The Faith that had saved her. Eventually she'd earned her place here, in the organization that hid behind the facade of the Institute for Cultural Studies.

Revelation.

The moment Tess walked through the doors, she could feel the security cameras on her. This was no ordinary college.

As Tess touched her hands on the fingerprint readers and looked into the iris-scanner, she could feel the receptionist's gaze on her.

"Welcome back, Tess."

Gone was the normal cool indifference. There was a respect in the receptionist's voice that Tess had never heard before.

"They're expecting you downstairs."

Downstairs. That was a first too. Only the inner circle were allowed there. "Do I need an access code?"

"No. You're cleared now. Just touch the pads."

Everything really *had* changed.

The building was a brilliant mix of old and new. Underneath the roof, with its massive iron girders, was a large communal area where everyone ate together. Lining the brick walls were glass cubicles; on the ground floor these were briefing and preparation rooms and on the upper floors there were bedrooms where the students lived.

As she walked along the central gantry, a girl of her own age with a crazy mass of curly hair hurried towards her.

"Tess! All anyone can talk about is *you*." Erin's voice was a mixture of admiration and disbelief. "Are you going to a safe house for a while?"

"I think they've got another assignment for me."

"Already?"

Tess glanced down into the dining area and saw the uneasy looks in the other students' eyes. She was no longer one of them. The Metro bomb had pushed her across some invisible threshold.

"I don't want to be late," Tess said, feeling suddenly uncomfortable.

"Sure." Erin stepped aside. "I'll come and see you after."

The strangeness followed Tess down into the vaulted basement, where Blackwood and 5 members of the Suprema were waiting. Tess only knew them by sight as they were too high up in Revelation to have any dealings with ordinary students; yet now each in turn stepped forwards to embrace her.

"By the Gift of the Creator."

"By the Gift of the Creator."

They whispered the words to her like a blessing, wrapping Tess in a cloak of heroism.

Then they all got down to the ruthless business of fighting for The Faith.

# 19

Cillian had never seen so many people in the apartment. While one paramedic dressed his head wound, another filed the injury report; beyond them 2 uniformed police were questioning the security guard from the Spire's Cockpit who had seen the chase on CCTV and called the emergency services. Over by the window-wall, prying with professional deftness, was Detective Qin.

"You're certainly having a rough week," Qin said, his curious eyes dancing around the room. "First the Metro, then this..."

Cillian looked at him in disbelief, angry that he should be so flippant.

"I checked your records," Qin went on, unperturbed. "You've never been the victim of crime, then in a couple of days... "

"What exactly are you saying?"

"The timing's suspicious."

"How can you think they're related?"

"You ever come across any radical groups at university?"

"No!" Cillian didn't try to hide his incredulity.

"What about religious factions?"

"Right now I'm working on the rotational properties of 5-dimensional objects. You really think I'd have any interest in religion?"

"Why the attitude? I'm trying to help."

"Can't we do this another time?"

"Now is good." Qin waved the paramedics aside so that he could focus more intently on Cillian. "You must've been hiding *something* in here. It was a professional job – the intruder knew exactly what security you had and how to get around it." He pointed to the electronic box that one of the uniforms was removing from the Main Control Unit. "That Disabler – we normally only see those in commercial espionage."

"I've no idea what he was looking for."

"He didn't steal any tech?"

"No."

"Valuables?"

"No."

"You see anything obvious that's missing?"

Cillian glanced around the room, but everything seemed to be in its place.

"Don't you think that's strange?" Qin persisted.

"Lots of things are strange right now. Too many."

"Yeah ... I certainly know that feeling."

Qin crossed the room and picked up a toolkit. "He brought this with him. Almost like he was planning to do some DIY."

Cillian looked at the toolkit: screwdrivers, spanners, a set of blades; it was the sort of thing you could pick up at any hardware store.

"Ideas?"

"I don't know." Cillian shook his head wearily. "It doesn't make sense."

Qin drummed his fingers on the toolkit as he put it down. "Have you always had a bad temper?"

"What? I don't."

"Could've fooled me." Qin picked up the CyberSpecs that were now sealed in a plastic evidence bag. "You really went for him."

Cillian felt suddenly uneasy as he realized that the whole encounter had been captured on the Specs.

"Seems to me like he was searching, not stealing," Qin said. "Until you interrupted." He touched the pad on the side of the Specs. "It's an ugly scene."

Cillian watched as the video replayed on the lenses. He saw his hands slamming the intruder into the wall, crushing his skull. It was sickening to see the look of violent rage on his own face.

"Wouldn't have marked you down as such an aggressive type," Qin observed drily.

"He was in my home!"

"He could've had a knife. You didn't know. You just went for him. Maths student becomes have-a-go hero." Qin tossed the Specs back onto the table. "Almost as if you were trying to protect something."

"I was frightened."

Qin crouched down and gazed at him searchingly. "What was he looking for?"

"I wish I knew." Cillian put his head in his hands, struggling to think clearly, frustrated by all these events that refused to fit into a pattern.

The doorbell rang and more officials filed in.

It was going to be a long afternoon.

# 20

When the police finally left, Cillian clambered into the shower and turned everything on to full blast. The hot jets pummelled his body from all directions and he closed his eyes, lost in momentary oblivion.

Without warning he started to tremble, as the shock finally caught up with him. He gripped the shower head tightly, desperately trying to steady himself.

If only his father was here, he would know how to handle this, what to do next—

But Paul was dead.

Dead, yet refusing to completely die.

Uncontrollable spasms suddenly wracked Cillian's body, as if he was going to vomit up all his insides.

What was happening to him?

Was he having some kind of breakdown?

The alarming energy that had surged through his veins when he attacked the intruder – where had that come from? And worse, why had he enjoyed the dangerous feeling of power?

Cillian forced himself to breathe deeply until the trembling passed. He flipped the jets from water to hot air to dry off, then walked back through to the lounge.

The victim support counsellor had left her card on the table; was that what he needed? Counselling? Was all this part of some strange post-traumatic stress?

Maybe.

But would opening up to a police counsellor just make him more vulnerable? He had the sense that Qin knew more than he was saying, just like the doctor at the hospital.

Something else was going on – Cillian was sure of it. Forces were shifting beneath the glossy surface of everyday life, like those underground rivers that flowed deep beneath the City, slithering past in the darkness.

Cillian tossed the card back on the table. He didn't need counselling; he needed things to fit into a pattern.

# 21

"Everything we've learnt about him has confirmed my suspicions," Blackwood said, as photos of Cillian appeared on the WallScreen in the basement briefing room.

He scrolled through numerous pictures plucked from social media. "He's living proof that Foundation City has crossed a line."

"We must stop this abomination," one of the Suprema, a woman with heavy-rimmed glasses, pronounced.

Tess looked at the pictures on the screen. "Shouldn't we wait?"

"Wait?"

Tess could hear the surprise in Blackwood's voice – students never questioned the Suprema. "To see if the City has learnt from the Metro attack," she went on. "Now people know how serious we are, shouldn't we give them time to change their minds?"

"*When I reflected on his crimes and malice,*" Glasses quoted the *Frankenstein* text by heart, "*my hatred and revenge burst all bounds of moderation."*

Tess glanced at the rest of the Suprema, hoping for discussion rather than decree, but no-one was going to contradict Glasses.

"The thing is," Blackwood said, striking a more pragmatic tone, "with Cillian exposed, his controllers will want to pull him off the streets. So we have to work fast. For some time we've known that an organization called P8 has been funding radical research, incubating dangerous ideas." He turned and gazed at the picture of Cillian emerging from the smoke-filled station. "This suggests they've gone way beyond that. Cillian should've died in that inferno, but he walked out *unscathed."*

"In Foundation City, everything has a price, but nothing has value any more," Glasses said. "Not even the human soul."

Tess studied the photograph, willing herself to forget that *she* was the one who had put the grief on Cillian's face. "I think he knows the value of the human soul."

"It's not just about him, though." Blackwood looked searchingly at Tess. "My fear is about Generation Zero."

"You have no proof of that," Glasses said impatiently.

"But it makes sense," Blackwood retorted. "There's no point creating just one."

"Right now we have to deal with what's in front of us, not wild theories." Glasses turned to Tess. "You need to reach out to Cillian. Win his trust. Then use him to cut open the heart of P8."

"Haven't we shed enough blood?" Tess said.

"It's because we're trying to *stop* blood being shed that you have to do this."

"Maybe you should choose one of the other operators," Tess said quietly.

"No." Blackwood crossed the room and sat down next to her. "It has to be you."

"After everything that's happened?"

"*Because* of everything that's happened. You're upset. Of course you are. Which is why you need to see *up close* what we're really fighting against."

Tess looked at the picture of Cillian holding his dying father.

"Don't underestimate him, Tess. There was a time when people killed each other just because of the colour of their skin. What P8 are doing will divide humanity all over again. Only this time it'll be for ever. People are sleepwalking into this, and it's fallen to us to wake them up."

92. 93. 94.

The pull-ups were really hurting now, but Tess refused to stop. She had to keep going until all the doubts in her mind were quashed.

The iron beam she gripped ran across the width of her room, so she could look at the WallScreen as she worked out. She'd selected images of Cillian to try to get into his mind, but there was something distant and inscrutable about him that was locking her out. Maybe it was that his face was a little bit too symmetrical, or maybe it was the strange sense of composure that surrounded him even in the middle of trauma. The only way in seemed to be through his eyes, which were flecked with vulnerability.

Tess dropped to the floor and strapped some weights to her ankles.

Vulnerable meant easy, *if* you could harden your heart.

She leapt up to do another 100 pull-ups, trammelling her mind on to a single track: the mission.

# 22

Cillian sat down at the workstation in his father's study and placed the encryption-tab on a glass reader. Moments later the wraparound screen came to life, exactly as Paul had left it on the morning he died.

On the right, the latest news about the looming City elections; next to that, a discussion forum where his father had been having a heated debate with someone about new Transport Zones. Further around the glass curve was a message from Bond Street Barbers – they'd had to move Paul's appointment because some builders had cut through a power cable and they had no hot water.

There was a to do list.

A quote from a holiday company.

Scribbled notes from a book he'd been reading—

Cillian closed his eyes. This wasn't helping. He had to focus or he'd be swallowed up by the past.

Follow the money. Wasn't that what the police always did on TV?

He opened his father's bank accounts and his eyes darted over the transactions scrolling up the screen. Immediately his mathematical mind engaged, hunting for patterns, searching for rhythms in the way money ebbed and flowed—

*I see it.*

The first anomaly: the salary from the Walk-In clinic wasn't his father's only income; someone else was paying him too.

At first glance it looked like irregular amounts at random intervals; 1st January, 1st February, 2nd March, 3rd May, 5th August, 13th August, 8th May, 5th March, 3rd February, 2nd January. And then it repeated.

*I see it.*

1,1,2,3,5,8,13,8,5,3,2,1.

The first 7 numbers of the Fibonacci sequence on a loop. Nothing random about it at all.

Cillian tapped *payee details* but they'd been withheld. He sent a clearance request, the bank pinged the computer to check its identity, the encryption-tab bounced back a security code and the next level was unlocked.

Gilgamesh.

On each of the dates in the sequence a payment had been made to his father from *Gilgamesh P8.*

Quickly Cillian scrolled back through the accounts; year after year the money had been coming in, going all the way back—

16 years. To the very month Cillian was born. The start of the sequence. Somehow he and the money were inextricably linked.

Somehow.

Had he ever been to Gilgamesh? Was he born there?

He clicked the *family* icon. Whole chunks of his

father's archives were devoted to Cillian: all the emails he'd ever sent, school reports and projects, swimming certificates, thousands of photos and videos, everything from ice cream by the river, to nervous rollerblading, to the school play—

And suddenly Cillian saw the second anomaly. No matter where he looked in the digital archive, there was nothing before his third birthday.

*Nothing.*

# 23

*The Bigger Yellow. Because some things you don't want to let go.*

The strapline was emblazoned across the vast underground warehouse in glowing letters, and business was booming. For all the brilliance of the virtual world, people still cherished real objects; they just didn't have room for them in their homes.

A huge glass funnel collected light from the surface and piped it down to a grid of walkways leading off the atrium. Even though it meant there were no dark corners, the long deserted corridors still felt a bit eerie, which was why egg-shaped Security-Bots patrolled and polished 24/7. Remembering his fight with the intruder, Cillian wondered how effective the bots would actually be in the heat of battle, but they looked official enough, and were decked with flashing lights that exuded a reassuring sense of authority.

4610-7 was his father's unit, at the far end of Corridor

23. As Cillian walked towards it he passed some strange characters shuffling around their units like troglodytes: an old woman surrounded by files, chuckling to herself; a couple of geeky men packing model trains into cardboard boxes for shipping; a young woman scrubbing and disinfecting her empty unit as if something dreadful had leaked.

Finally Cillian stopped, checked the unit number and undid the heavy padlock. He rolled up the shutter to reveal stacks of plastic boxes with faded labels, all in his father's neat handwriting.

He lifted down "Childhood Drawings", opened the lid and inhaled the smell of old paper and faded paint. Memories flooded back ... walking excitedly home from school proudly clutching paintings he'd done, then seeing them perched on the bookshelves.

Quickly he popped the lids off more boxes: school exercise books, cherished posters that had decorated his bedroom walls, his first football kit...

And yet *still* there was nothing from before his third birthday.

"Archived Photos". There must at least be a photograph. Every parent has a picture of them holding their newborn baby.

He flung the lid off and started rifling through envelopes stuffed full of photos, digging deep, searching for the oldest ones.

In frustration he tipped the box up, spewing envelopes across the concrete floor, then dropped to his knees. His hands quickly sorted everything into date order even though his guts already feared the truth...

There was nothing from before his third birthday.

Not a *single* photograph.

It was as if he'd just sprung into existence.

# 24

Tess never failed to be dismayed when she came to one of the City's traditional churches.

For 900 years the ancient bells of All-Hallows had echoed across the landscape, summoning the faithful to tramp through muddy streets in search of salvation. But its sturdy stone walls belonged to a time when Earth was the centre of the universe, and when the Creator ruled the lives of men without question. Now The Faith had been hollowed out into little more than a social convention. Its beautiful buildings were still handy for births, marriages and deaths, but its bells echoed off steel and glass shrines to money and technology, the real gods of Foundation City.

Today the Great and Good had gathered for a memorial service for all the victims of the Metro crash; in Tess's eyes it just made the hypocrisy worse.

She watched with disdain as politicians and heavy-hitters arrived. It infuriated her to see how they all lined up to express their outrage to the hungry press pack about the "fanatical actions of extremists". But not one politician dared acknowledge that Revelation might be waging a legitimate war on the moral corruption festering at the heart of the City. Not one argued that The Faith *should* be a religion of action that fought for justice and for those who really paid the price for the City's wealth.

Anyone saying things like that would soon find themselves on a security watch list. So much for the freedom of speech that Foundation liked to boast about.

Even when the service started, the profanity didn't end. Everyone muted their smartCells but couldn't bear to turn them off. Tess saw that instead of remembering the dead, people were checking their screens every few seconds. No doubt they were pinging each other's social feeds to see if there was networking to be done here, deals to be struck or money to be made.

"If you wouldn't mind?" a voice whispered.

Tess turned and saw one of the vergers offering her the DigiPlate, a circle of pulsing LEDs on a steel disc. *Touch your smartCell to donate. Thank you for giving generously.*

She swiped her screen across the reader and passed it down the line. Right now she wasn't here to make a point, but to blend in.

And to lock on to her target.

Tess watched the DigiPlate as it was handed from person to person ... studying each face in turn ... searching for the one that was too perfectly symmetrical...

# 25

Even though he wasn't religious, Cillian found the memorial service strangely comforting. He closed his eyes and sat absolutely still, letting music from the massive organ wash over him, immersing himself in the sound of the echoing choir. For one hour it was a chance to remember all the good things about his father and forget the disturbing anomalies that had opened up since his death.

But as a chord swelled for the closing hymn, Cillian felt someone's gaze on him.

He snapped open his eyes, senses bristling ... and saw her. A teenage girl was sitting in the opposite wing of the transept – strong, angular face with sharp eyes staring directly at him, intent and unblinking.

Cillian glared back defiantly, expecting her to look away.

But she didn't.

Something about her seemed out of place in this church, and when she did finally break the moment, it wasn't with eyes darting furtively down to a smartCell, it was to look up at a huge painted icon that loomed over the altar. Cillian followed her gaze. She was taking in every detail of the muscles tensed in pain, the blood trickling down fragile skin, the horror of that violent death.

The words of the final blessing were barely out of the priest's mouth when the congregation broke rank in a bustle of pent-up chatter and coughing.

Cillian let the worst of the crush go, then pulled his coat on and filed out into the blast of freezing air and flashguns. Instinctively he veered to the side, heading for one of the alleys to avoid the worst of the media scrum, when unexpectedly he found himself walking straight towards the girl from the church. She was standing at the top of the steps, waiting for him.

He slowed his pace. "Do I know you?"

"No." She continued staring at him.

"Only in church, I thought—"

"You're being played," Tess said, glancing back at the crowds milling outside All-Hallows. "By them."

"Who *are* you?"

"That's why you're smart not to trust them."

"I'm sorry ... I think you've got the wrong person."

But as he turned to go she reached out and gripped his arm. "I can help you, Cillian. That's why I'm here."

Suddenly he felt very uneasy. "Leave me alone, please. I don't know what you're talking about."

"P8. And your father."

The words hit him in the guts.

"You're through the looking glass now," Tess said quietly. "I should know. I've been there most of my life."

"What about my father? What do you know?"

They heard a flutter of laughter and saw some of the people from the service heading towards them.

"We shouldn't talk here," Tess said. She went to take his hand, but Cillian pulled away. "Look, you can spend the rest of your life skating across the surface, or you can find out what's really going on. Your choice." She turned away and hurried down the steps towards Constitution Square.

Cillian's instincts were urging him not to trust her – she was a complete stranger. But what did that count for now? Hadn't his own father turned into a stranger?

3 more steps and she'd be out of sight.

And he might never get answers.

"Wait!"

She stopped, turned back and smiled.

# 26

"When I was 6 years old, everyone I knew died."

As she spoke, Tess looked out across the square, where crowds had come to see huge waves rolling across the sides of buildings; not adverts, but video art sponsored by one of the banks.

"They were killed by a virus. The Derespino Pandemic," she said starkly.

A jumble of TV news images flashed into Cillian's mind. "Wasn't that in the Provinces?"

"I'm not from the City, not originally." Tess took a swig of cappuccino from her paper cup. "Derespino arrived from nowhere. Without warning. I remember it was a Saturday morning when the first person fell sick. I'd been out riding my bike. It was a beautiful sunny day, and as I cycled back into the village, I saw this huddle of people. Someone had collapsed. He was lying on the ground, struggling to breathe. There was blood coming from his mouth ... I'd never seen anyone look so grey. He died in front of me, there on the street. And once it had started, it tore through everything: villages, farms, schools."

"I thought they found a cure?"

Tess shook her head. "The virus was drug resistant. So they just fenced us in, sealed off hundreds of square kilometres, then sat back and waited until people stopped dying. 80 of us survived. Out of 5,000. When help finally came, they found me locked in an attic with a few crumbs of food and the dregs of water in a saucepan. My parents had locked me in there to try to keep me safe; when they knew they were infected, they couldn't think what else to do."

"I'm sorry," Cillian said, disturbed at the way this stranger was opening up to him. "To go through that..."

"On the TV it was all 'brave medics in protective suits, risking their lives to save innocent people'. That was just one of the lies. Something wasn't right about the whole outbreak. Even though I was just a kid, I *knew* they were lying."

"About what?"

"Everything. For months afterwards I couldn't stop thinking about the crop-dusters; it was like they were haunting me. The fields around our village were always being sprayed – that wasn't new. But the last time they did it ... the spray hung in the air for hours. We could see rainbows all over the place, hundreds of them. As kids we thought it was magic, but..." Tess fell silent.

"You really think someone poisoned you? Deliberately?"

"Not think, *know*. We were lab rats. They put the survivors in quarantine, and they subjected us to every test imaginable, every scan, every examination. For months."

"To make sure you were safe?"

"To find out *why* we'd survived. What did we have that the others didn't? *That's* how they found the cure."

"So it was all some kind of medical trial?" Cillian was struggling to comprehend the scale of what she was saying.

"When they'd finished, they turfed us out and forgot about us. 3 years ago there was a Derespino outbreak in the Far East, remember? Foundation City had the only vaccine. They supplied drugs for 2 billion people. Half a trillion dollars' worth. You tell me if that's not worth killing for."

Cillian studied her face, trying to work out how far trust could stretch. All his senses were telling him that she was genuine – her open expression, her steady gaze. But she was talking about conspiracy and murder on a massive scale.

"When I saw that picture of you walking out of the Metro," Tess leant closer, "I had the same feeling. You shouldn't have survived, but you did. Just like me. We're both outsiders."

Cillian looked away. "Last week I'd have said you were paranoid."

"But now?"

He said nothing.

"Things are unravelling because you're not like other people," Tess said. "I'm guessing you never have been."

Part of Cillian wanted to pull away, but another part knew that if he didn't open up to someone, he would implode.

He gazed out across the square, absorbing the dynamics of the crowd—

*I see it.*

"Those people over there, by the fountain."

Tess followed his gaze and noticed that the crowd had spontaneously formed itself into one-way lanes, like flowing currents.

"In 8 seconds, the direction's going to flip."

"What?"

"Just watch."

She studied the crowds ... and moments later was astonished to see the flows spasm, collapse into random, then re-form, moving in the *opposite* direction.

"How did you know that?" she whispered.

"The world is flooded with information, staggering amounts of it pouring out all the time. There's so much, it's impossible to process. But I've got this ... ability to sense patterns. I can see them like shapes in a landscape. And if you look closely enough at the present, if you really see what's going on, you can predict the future."

"That's incredible," Tess said.

"Means you never get stuck in the slowest queue."

Tess laughed. "Useful."

"My father knew what I could do from when I was young. He nurtured it. Only now ... it turns out there were secrets as well. A whole chunk of my life is missing ... and he was getting money."

"From P8."

"How did you know?" He looked at her, unnerved.

"That's how they work. They buy people off."

"Who are *they*? I can't find anything on the Net."

"You won't. They're too smart for that."

"Then I'll never get to the truth, not now my father's..." His voice trailed off, struggling with the brutal finality of the word "dead".

Tess put her hand on his arm. "P8 funds dangerous science. It meddles with things it doesn't fully understand,

and everyone else pays the price. If your father was getting money from P8, then you're not safe any more."

"So do you think he was trying to warn me? Should I go into hiding or something?"

"You have to fight."

"Tess, I'm a maths student—"

"All these years I've been training myself, getting stronger. Learning to fight without knowing exactly *who* to fight. But you're smart; you can figure it out."

"I'm way out of my depth."

"Cillian, I need justice for what happened to my parents, and I know you can help me. I've been waiting for someone like you."

He felt the intensity of her gaze on him. "The virus, the payments, my father – you really think it's all related?"

"Don't you?"

"Something is very screwed up." Cillian shook his head. "I know that much."

"Then let's un-screw it. The two of us."

It was compelling how simple she made it sound. Finally here was someone who said exactly what she thought, who didn't try to hide behind half-truths.

"You really think we'll get far?"

"Absolutely." Tess stood up and tossed her empty coffee cup into a bin.

# 27

The Bullet Train was barely out of Foundation City when the gales kicked up, howling across the open landscape, tearing through the black fingers of winter trees.

Tess gazed through the train's panoramic glass roof and saw some police surveillance drones heading back to base. They couldn't fly in these conditions, which left the Provinces pretty much unprotected during bad weather. Not that there were many people out here to protect. The endless snowfields were dotted with massive domed farms, where satellite-controlled machines ploughed and planted and harvested day and night. Although small teams of engineers kept everything working, it was machines that really fed Foundation City. Scattered communities did still exist, mainly people who had dropped out of City life, but they kept themselves to themselves. Beyond the Northern Hub, the leisure resorts took care of security by simply fencing in whole mountains.

"You're sure this is the right place to start?" Cillian

asked as he watched the lights of the City recede in the gloaming.

"I'm sure," Tess replied.

"Only, I thought everything was run from the City now."

"It might be controlled there, but the things they want to hide, things that are a bit off the scale ... that happens in the Provinces."

Cillian heard the note of warning in her voice. "Doesn't it worry you? Coming back after what happened?"

Tess looked out of the window. The train line was running next to the Great Canal, where convoys of massive barges were taking the City's trash for recycling and disposal. "Life's cheaper out here. That's just the way it is. But maybe that's going to help us."

"Very reassuring." Cillian laughed nervously.

With a gentle tilt, the Bullet Train peeled away from the canal and headed over the Viaducts, crossing vast tracts that had been flooded to create reservoirs.

Tess glanced at her smartCell. "See? We really are on our own now."

Cillian checked the screen as one by one all the networks dropped away.

"At least whatever we do out here, we won't be leaving traces on the Net."

"It's weird though." As he glanced around the carriage, Cillian realized he wasn't the only one to feel anxious; a group of college students heading north on a ski trip were joking loudly, flipping the windows onto entertainment mode, trying to block out the rawness of the Provinces.

"What was it really like? Living out here?"

The question caught Tess off guard. "No-one's normally interested."

"It must've felt like being on a different planet."

"It felt free, I suppose. Maybe it's because I was a kid, but we did things that no-one in the City does – ran wild in the forests, spent whole days building pebble dams." The memories fluttered back to her. "Seems like a long way off now."

"Certainly a long way from my childhood."

"I bet you were all online gaming and social surfing?"

Cillian laughed. "Guilty."

"No wonder you got on a Fast-Track."

"I don't know about that."

"You must've made a small fortune, second-guessing stocks and shares with your sixth sense, or whatever you call it."

"I wish. It doesn't work like that; there are too many hiddens in financial markets."

Tess fired him a sceptical look. "But that's a pretty expensive university you're at."

"I came up with this app for putting together the perfect online football team. It was just for me and some mates, but it took off. Next thing, a bank got to hear about it and applied it to their own management."

"That's crazy."

"It's how I got sponsored for uni."

"We come from pretty different worlds, you and me."

"Maybe..." Cillian pointed out of the window at an imposing saw-toothed ridge connecting 3 huge peaks. "But in a million years, all that'll be left of Foundation City will be a thin band of dark rock in the side of a mountain. And no-one will know any different."

"Don't go all weird on me."

"I think it's comforting. We're just passing through."

"No, it's bleak."

Tess watched him stare intently at the granite mountains. Suddenly he became unnaturally still and focussed, as if his whole being had locked on to something. His hands lay flat on the small table, the fingers perfectly spaced; his eyes seemed to blink a little too slowly, and his breathing was unnervingly steady and controlled. Tess shuddered as she remembered the Suprema's ominous description: *an abomination*. Deep down, there really was something unknowable about Cillian. He seemed normal on the surface, but a part of him was beating to an entirely different rhythm. You just had to know what to look for.

"What happened to your mother, Cillian?"

He snapped out of his reverie. "I never knew her. She died when I was born."

"I'm sorry."

"It's always just been me and my..." Then he remembered the brutal truth. That was in the past, now he was alone.

Tess felt guilt rising in her guts like burning acid. She closed her eyes and clenched her fists, digging her nails into her palms.

"Are you OK?" Cillian reached across the table. "Tess?"

She opened her eyes quickly.

"What's wrong?"

"Nothing."

Cillian looked at her searchingly.

"It's these tilting trains. They make me feel a bit sick."

"Here..." He swiped the window to replace the landscape with an interactive display. "That should help."

"You have to close the door on pain, Cillian. I learnt that the hard way. It's the only way to deal with it."

He nodded. "My father was the one thing I thought I

knew. The fixed point. But I was wrong."

"The only thing you can really rely on is yourself," Tess said. "Your own strength."

The doors at the far end of the carriage slid open and 2 armed police officers strolled in. Uniformed patrols had been doubled right across the City in the days since the Metro attack. Tess knew it was little more than theatre, designed to reassure people that something was being done; the real policing was all intelligence-led, and Revelation was a master at staying hidden in the system.

Nevertheless she felt on edge, and she knew the police were trained to spot signs of anxiety.

"I'm just going to freshen up," she said. "Would you call the Buffet-Bot? I could murder a coffee."

"The doughnuts on these trains are legendary," Cillian said, pulling up the food menu.

"Why not?" She smiled.

As the bathroom door sighed shut, Tess double-clicked the locks. Immediately a soft voice welcomed her to the sanitary-pod and started guiding her through instructions for how to get *"the most refreshing and hygienic experience—"*

She hit *Mute*.

Focus. Deception was her job. She'd been trained to lie, to hold cover.

The closer she let him get to her, the easier her job would become. That was all that mattered. Getting the job done.

She saw a bar running across the pod ceiling and leapt up, grabbing it with both hands.

1, 2, 3…

Revelation was the truth.

6, 7, 8...
Foundation City was the corruption.
11, 12, 13...
P8 was the enemy.
16, 17, 18...
To be true to The Faith meant to follow.

# 28

Cillian gazed up at the interlocking glass curves of the station roof as the Bullet Train pulled into the Northern Hub. Even though it was an outpost of civilization, the Hub was trying hard to feel metropolitan.

"We'd better be quick. Unless you want to queue for hours," Tess said, leading the way off the train.

They stood on the platform for a few moments, trying to get their bearings. Most of the passengers hurried away in search of shuttles to take them further north to the leisure parks; slower off the train were the older people who had made their money in Foundation and retired to the quieter life of the coastal resorts. Coming in the opposite direction was a steady stream of teenagers with bulging suitcases, boarding the train to go in search of wealth and opportunity in the City. Tess couldn't help feeling sorry for them. They had no idea about the tough reality awaiting them, the intense competition that would burn so many dreams away. She wondered how long it would be before all that bright optimism in their eyes evaporated.

"Over there." Cillian spotted an illuminated sign above the main concourse: *Hospital Shuttles.* Large flashing arrows pointed to several different exits.

As they got closer, Tess and Cillian realized that hundreds of people – some bandaged, others on crutches, at least a dozen in wheelchairs – all had the same idea. They were converging on the shuttle pick-up points, where buses loaded and dropped off in a continuous stream.

"Looks like Gilgamesh is big business," Tess said, taken aback.

"It's the only hospital in the Northern Province," Cillian replied grimly. "No Walk-Ins out here."

They managed to get a seat near the back of the shuttle, and sat quietly as the bus pushed into the empty landscape. Cillian gazed out of the window. The only road the snowploughs kept clear was the one that led to Gilgamesh; all the others seemed to have vanished under ice.

Tess's eyes darted around, checking out the other passengers, wondering what illness each of them was battling. They all sat, patient and uncomplaining, quietly convinced that Gilgamesh would restore them and end their pain. It reminded Tess of a history textbook she'd once read about people going on a pilgrimage to Lourdes in search of miracle cures, only here science was the religion.

"They didn't take any prisoners when they built those," Cillian said.

Tess followed his gaze. They were passing through a massive wind farm, hundreds and hundreds of spinning turbines lined up like a steel battalion.

"I think it was a town. Once." Cillian pointed to a strange pattern of scars in the ground.

With a jolt Tess recognized the imprint of a vanished community. Houses, roads, shops had all been bulldozed in one swoop to make way for this wind farm. People had been moved out, and all that was left were thousands of lines in the ground where the snow struggled to settle. "They certainly do things differently in the Provinces."

20 minutes later the bus slowed down and stopped by some bulldozers that were blocking the road.

"Sorry about the delay, folks," the driver said cheerily over the tannoy. "Storm last week took out the bridge. Never seen rain like it. Went on for 3 days."

Everyone craned their heads to get a better look. The pillars under the bridge had been washed clean away, leaving a twisted steel skeleton half-submerged in the icy water. Dozens of men in orange overalls were hard at work, digging the soggy mud and clearing tarmac that had been ripped up like bits of cardboard.

The shuttle bus was hitched to a couple of tractors, and as it was towed across a temporary pontoon bridge, Cillian saw what was really going on.

"Bloody hell..." The men doing the hard labour were chained to each other with manacles around their feet. "Chain gangs? *Literally?*"

"You never wondered why Foundation City is so safe?"

"I knew the prisons were in the Provinces but..."

"Everyone has to earn their keep. Even convicts. When they say crime is sorted –" Tess pointed at the miserable, frozen souls knee-deep in mud – "*that's* what they mean."

\*\*\*

It was a relief to finally arrive at Gilgamesh, a vast, sprawling complex that felt like a glowing beacon in the wilderness.

"This is a hell of a lot bigger than I'd imagined," Tess said, looking up at the emergency helicopters landing on the roof.

"Apparently there's been a hospital here for 1,000 years."

"I can believe it."

At the heart of the complex was a gothic fortress, all spires, steep roofs and cloistered courtyards built on spectacular granite cliffs overlooking the ocean. But it looked like numerous layers had been added across the centuries, the most recent one wrapping the hospital in an ultra-modern glass skin.

"Did you feel that?" Cillian asked pensively.

"What?"

"Through your feet."

Tess concentrated, but couldn't feel anything.

Cillian crouched down and rested his hand on the cold ground. "There..."

Tess did the same, placing her hand next to his. A few moments later she felt a tremor through her palm, a deep resonant *thump* from inside the earth.

"It's the sea," Cillian said. "The waves pounding the rocks."

It was like an ancient heartbeat, a primal pulse underneath all the gloss and technology.

Cillian looked up at Gilgamesh. What was it about this place that had seared itself into his father's mind?

## 29

*"Patient? Visitor? Or new staff?"*

The Orientation Buggies waiting inside the main entrance were as polite and diligent as the day they were programmed. Cillian touched *Visitor* as he and Tess climbed into one of the small pods, and the tour started.

It was a great way to get the lie of the land without arousing suspicion. The OB whisked them down corridors and up ramps, gliding past other buggies with perfect timing, attentively stopping to give patients being wheeled on stretchers the right of way. While the OB blithely rattled off facts and figures about the hospital and how many people it treated every week, Cillian and Tess studied the buildings, looking for anything suspicious or out of place.

But all they saw were endless corridors and wards that looked identical.

"This is going to take for ever," Tess sighed. "Can't you

do your pattern recognition thing? Find something that doesn't fit?"

Cillian touched the buggy's screen to pull up an interactive map, and paged through the different levels. It unnerved Tess to see how he changed when he locked into that mode. It was almost tangible – a weird energy seemed to surround him, excluding everything else.

"The patterns of the old building are so confused," he said, shaking his head. "It's all a bit of a mess."

"Then let's go for the most obscure part." Tess touched *Asthma Clinic*. "No-one gets that any more."

The OB took a sharp left and headed off on the new course. After a few minutes, the corridors started to get narrower, then a set of doors slid back and the buggy crossed a glassed-in walkway between 2 surgical wings.

"This is more like it." Tess hit *Pause* and the buggy pulled smoothly to a stop.

From here you could look down on to the oldest parts of Gilgamesh: forbidding granite towers clustered around a swathe of open ground that led down to the sheer cliff edge.

"What about those old buildings? What happens in there?"

*"The original hospital buildings are only used for storage now,"* the OB replied. *"Over the years people have suggested they could be turned into a museum, but there are no plans at present."*

Cillian and Tess exchanged a sceptical look. "All that for storage?" she whispered. "I don't think so."

There was a massive construction project underway, with cranes and excavators and piling machines reaching deep into the heart of the old structure. Looms of cable were unspooling from huge drums, equipment cabinets were being lowered through roofs and the whole site was bristling with security cameras.

But as Cillian climbed out of the buggy to take some pictures, the OB suddenly got edgy.

*"Please get back in the vehicle."*

"I won't be a minute—"

*"Return to your seat—"*

"OK. I heard the first time—"

*"This is not an authorized stop. Return to the vehicle."*

"Relax! Take it easy." Cillian climbed back on board before the OB flipped out. "Are you always such a nag?" All he got back was a sulky silence.

"Must've touched a nerve," Tess said quietly. She hit *Resume* on the control panel and they trundled off, the OB instantly in a good mood again.

*"Coming up on our left is the Eye Unit with its specialist operating theatres for retinal surgery..."*

But Cillian and Tess weren't paying attention. They looked back at the old buildings disappearing from view. *That* was the Gilgamesh they were interested in.

# 30

They got the Orientation Buggy to drop them at the hospital library, where one of the archivists seemed keen to help.

"We're very proud of our medical school," she said. "Generations of doctors have trained here. Can your father remember his login codes?"

"No. He..." Suddenly Cillian dried up. He hadn't thought the lie through.

"He was in an accident," Tess swooped in.

"I'm sorry to hear that," the archivist sympathized.

"That's why we're here. Cillian needs to find out things he never got to ask."

"Oh..." The archivist was suddenly embarrassed. "Of course." Anxious not to dwell on the awkwardness, she activated a reading card. "This is a day pass. All our records are on the system. It's pretty clear where to look."

Cillian and Tess chose a study-booth by the windows and drew up a couple of chairs. It didn't take them long to find the official records: his father's exam results all through med school, along with class photographs from each year. It was unnerving to see his father as a young man with long, curly hair and an easy smile.

"You kind of look like him," Tess said.

"It's strange, to see him there ... he had no idea what was going to happen, how his life was going to end."

Tess didn't want to go there. "Let's find out what happened to everyone else." She clicked the reverse image search and one by one, names appeared under each of the faces.

"Anyone familiar? Christmas cards? Social networks?"

Cillian swiped through the screens, but recognized no-one. "Maybe they all moved away."

Tess copied the list into the General Medical Database and hit search. Paul hadn't been the first in his class to die – one of the women had been killed in a jet ski accident 3 years after graduation. The rest were working in hospitals, mostly across Foundation City. A few were in the Far East.

But one person seemed to have vanished without trace: Conrad Herzog.

"Quite an achievement to disappear off the Net," Cillian said.

"Unless he never left." Tess typed Herzog's name into the Gilgamesh staff database. The cursor scrolled for a couple of seconds, then a *Restricted Access* page appeared.

"Bingo." Tess checked no-one was watching, then took out her smartCell and jumped a connection to the terminal.

"That doesn't look very legal," Cillian said apprehensively.

"It's a crawler. Looking for holes in their firewall."

"Useful."

"Very. That's why they banned them."

A meta-control screen appeared on the library terminal and Tess got to work, her fingers light and fast on the screen.

Cillian glanced around the library to see if they were being watched. A few days ago the idea of illegally hacking an official database would have filled him with horror, but a few days ago was a different world.

As it broke through, the crawler morphed into a branching database, pointing at individual file locations.

"Here we go..." Tess started tapping through the tangle of connections.

"Let me." Cillian tilted the screen towards him and relaxed his mind, letting his subconscious absorb the scrolling database—

When suddenly the screen froze. A beep, then the terminal shut down.

"Shit."

*"What are you doing?"*

They spun round and saw the archivist glaring at them.

"It crashed," Tess said innocently.

The archivist looked accusingly at Tess's smartCell, still connected to the terminal. "I think you'd better leave."

"We were just—"

"Before I call security."

"Calm down," Tess said, hurriedly stuffing her smart-Cell away.

"Just get out. Now."

# 31

"If he works at Gilgamesh, Herzog will have a car. We can find him through his number plate," Tess said as they walked briskly out of the main reception.

"Not on the hospital system. They'll have blocked us now."

"That's why we need one of *them*." She nodded towards a line of shabby taxis that had been repaired too many times. "They can always use a bit of extra cash."

As they climbed into the 4x4 at the front of the line, Tess leaned over the driver's seat. "Where's the nearest place to get online?"

"In there." The driver nodded towards the hospital.

"I mean privately online."

The taxi driver scrutinized her, wondering if he was being set up. "Depends how cunning you are, love."

"You'd be surprised." Tess reached inside her jacket, pulled out a wad of notes and placed them on the front armrest. "Unregistered dollars."

The taxi driver didn't flinch.

"You know they're worth twice the face value, right?"

The driver nodded. "I know." But still he didn't move.

Tess peeled off some more notes and tossed them down. "That's it," she said. "Take it or leave it."

The taxi driver slowly put the money into his pocket, then slipped the car into gear and drove them away from Gilgamesh.

As Tess sat back she saw Cillian staring at her, suspiciously. "What?"

"You really did come prepared."

"In another life, I should've been a boy scout."

They looked like simple chrome silos on stilts, deliberately minimalist to withstand the wild weather, but on the inside they were packed with meteorological instruments that spewed out streams of data to overhead satellites. As climate instability accelerated, the silos had sprung up right across the country in an attempt to protect Foundation City from hurricanes and ice storms. But for a sophisticated hacker, Tess informed Cillian, they provided plenty of bandwidth to freeload online.

The taxi driver parked far enough away to deny all knowledge, while Cillian and Tess crunched across the ice towards the silo.

"No way will you be able to hack a government database. Not with that." Cillian pointed at her smartCell.

"I don't need to. There's a mirror site on the Darknet."

"So we're rubbing shoulders with criminals and terrorists now?"

"It's the only place to surf without being snooped." She started tapping intently on her smartCell as they came within range.

Cillian looked up at the steel casing emblazoned with official logos. "If we carry on like this, sooner or later we're going to get caught."

"Do you want to find Herzog?" Tess said impatiently. "Or do you want to spend your whole life not knowing what's going on?"

"I'm just saying, we need to be careful." Cillian was taken aback by the sudden sharpness of her tone.

"Less worry, more faith … in *me*." A smile flashed across Tess's face, but now there was hardness in her eyes as well.

# 32

The grip of winter on the remote village was tight. Its freezing mists loomed around the buildings, lurked outside every door and window, enviously eyeing narrow cracks of light, searching for a way into the warmth.

Cillian and Tess huddled deeper into their coats as they walked past the gloomy houses.

"What do you suppose this place is like in summer?" Cillian ventured.

"Wet."

He laughed.

"Seriously. This is the sort of place that goes from freezing to wet, then straight back to freezing again."

Like most other villages, there were only 2 defining features here: the steeple of the old church, and the telecoms tower. But the church had long since become a relic; for the villagers all that mattered now was the telecoms tower, because that delivered the Ultranet into their homes.

"There's got to be more than this, hasn't there?" Tess shivered. "People shuttered up, whiling away their lives."

"It certainly depresses the hell out of me."

"How can they live so hollowed out? It's not right. It shouldn't be this way."

"Maybe that's why everyone wants to get out of the Provinces."

"As if it's much better in the City."

Cillian looked at her askance.

"It's true," Tess retorted. "Once you strip away all the noise and tech, life in Foundation's just as empty."

"You're not religious, are you?" Cillian asked warily.

"I don't worship profit and technology, if that's what you mean."

Cillian went very quiet.

"You can't tolerate that, can you?" Tess goaded. "Everything has to be rational. Explained. There's no room for the mysterious."

"The people who bombed the Metro did it in the name of religion. I can't tolerate *that*. At least science doesn't destroy lives."

"It destroyed mine," Tess said bluntly.

"That was money, not science."

"It's the same thing. Neither's interested in morality, in what's right and wrong. That gets forgotten every time." But immediately Tess sensed she'd said too much; she could feel Cillian's gaze scrutinizing her.

Keep calm.

Don't get drawn in.

Stick to the mission.

"We must be nearly there now." Tess checked the address on her smartCell. "That looks like it might be the place." She pointed to a large white building that had once been a farmhouse.

Cillian glanced at the car parked in front of the drive-way. "It's Herzog's registration."

Tess led the way up the path, banged on the front door and waited.

Footsteps inside, then a voice called out, "Who is it?"

Tess put her fingers to Cillian's lips to stop him reply-ing. "Sounds better coming from me," she whispered. Then calling through the door, "We're looking for Conrad Herzog."

A cautious silence.

The sound of bolts being slid back.

The door swung open to reveal a middle-aged man, tired eyes, a chaotic tangle of black hair. Guardedly, he looked Cillian and Tess up and down—

Then suddenly recognition hit him.

"Oh my god..." he whispered.

"I'm Paul's son."

Herzog nodded, stupefied. "I can see."

"And this is Tess."

Herzog glanced at her, then turned back to Cillian, staring at him intently.

"Can we come in?"

# 33

As Cillian talked, Tess studied Herzog. He listened with a dark intensity that was far more than curiosity; it was almost as if he was analysing Cillian, like a specimen.

All the while Herzog nodded slowly, but said nothing. Then finally, "Do you like sports?"

Cillian was nonplussed. "What's that got to do with anything?"

"Are you a good athlete? You look like you'd be pretty fast. Like it would come naturally."

"I've never been that interested." Cillian shrugged. "Why does it matter?"

"But you're an A* student, right?"

"Look, I came to find out about my father."

"More than A*," Herzog ventured. "Much more I bet."

"You want a CV or something?" Cillian was getting irritated by Herzog's evasiveness; but as he caught Tess's eye, she seemed to be urging him to tread carefully.

"I don't want to make trouble," Cillian said. "I just ...

how close were you as students?"

"We were friends."

"But you lost contact."

"It happens."

"Did you fall out? Was there an argument?"

"I guess."

Cillian could see deception written all over Herzog's face. "Whatever you know, why won't you just tell me?"

"I don't owe you any explanations. *He* was the one who cut himself off."

"What's so important about Gilgamesh?"

"Nothing."

"Then why did it mean so much to my father?"

"It's just another hospital."

"Bullshit." It was the first thing Tess had said since coming inside, and it really put Herzog on edge.

"What would *you* know?" he said defensively.

"I know when people are lying."

Herzog's eyes flicked between Tess and Cillian. "How exactly do you two know each other?"

"My father never told me about Gilgamesh until his dying breath," Cillian said, trying to keep him on track. "That must mean something. And now it turns out he was being paid money for the last 16 years. By Gilgamesh P8. Where you work."

Slowly Herzog tapped his teeth with his fingers. Cillian sensed that part of him was desperate to say more, to find out more ... but something was making him hold back. Fear, perhaps.

"Did he ever talk about your mother?" Herzog asked.

"She died when I was born. Did you know her?"

"That's a complicated question."

Cillian was confused. "No ... it's not."

"He'd been married to Natasha for 3 years when she was diagnosed with cancer. Of the heart – very rare. It was latent in her mother, second generation, but something triggered it. When they found out, Paul turned his whole life over to genetic research, desperately looking for some kind of radical cure." Herzog looked down as he remembered. "He was devastated. And angry. He couldn't accept she'd been cut down like that. You have to understand, the rage was going to eat him up unless he did something. That was Paul – always had to *do* something."

"So ... my mother fell pregnant even though she knew she was *dying*?"

"Like I said, it's not that simple."

"*When* did she die?" Tess cut hard across the doubletalk. "When? That's simple enough."

But her bluntness made Herzog back off. He stood up. "I really think you should leave now."

Cillian refused to move. "My father punched a hole in my life when he died. I shouldn't have to live with that. Why was he lying to me?"

"I've said all I can."

"Please ... you're the only one who can help."

"Natasha's buried here, in the village," Herzog reluctantly admitted. "I can take you to her grave. Maybe that's the best way."

# 34

One glance at the dates carved on the gravestone and Cillian's life twisted again. Natasha had been dead and buried 5 years before he was even born.

He turned to Herzog. "Why are you doing this to me?"

"I'm just telling you what I know—"

"Who the hell is Natasha?" Cillian felt the rage building inside.

"She was Paul's wife. But she wasn't your mother."

*"Then who was?"*

"I don't know!" Herzog said, hands raised. "Paul never told me. That's the truth, I swear."

Cillian looked down at the grave. The carved letters stared back at him defiantly.

"You OK?" Tess stepped closer, but Cillian pulled away.

A carved logo on the headstone caught his eye: *Chip-Enabled*. He took out his smartCell and scanned it over the logo.

Moments later a torrent of images played across his

screen: Natasha as a child, pictures of her growing up, video clips, fragments of music, tributes from friends, fleeting memories of her life. Cillian saw his father as a young man, hugging Natasha tightly. They looked so happy and easy – again he glimpsed that carefree side to his father, unconcerned with the worries of the world. It wasn't the man he had known at all.

The last image faded, leaving a 20th-century quote hanging on the screen: *Death is the seed from which I grow.*

"Grow what? What does it mean?"

Herzog looked at Tess. "Maybe you should ask *her.*"

"Stop playing games," Tess warned. "I know what you're trying to do."

"I'm sure you do. I bet you know a *lot* more."

"Please," Cillian said, "just tell us what you can."

Herzog hesitated – he could see the pain on Cillian's face. "Your father felt betrayed that Natasha couldn't be saved. It pushed him deeper into genetics ... the kind of research that frightens people. That's how he came into contact with P8. I can't say more than that."

"We've come a long way to get answers." Tess stepped towards him. "Do you seriously think we're just going to walk away?"

The coldness in her voice was a clear warning. Herzog tried to see if she had a weapon hidden under her coat, but he couldn't be sure.

"At first P8 was just a few labs," he continued reluctantly, "but it grew. Took over the old Gilgamesh buildings and sealed itself off from the rest of the hospital. They drew your father in, way too deep ... it put our friendship under strain. Then one day he just left. I never heard from him again."

"We need to get inside Gilgamesh," Tess said bluntly.

Herzog shook his head. "Impossible."

"And we need *you* to make it happen."

"Haven't you listened to a word I've said? There aren't any visiting hours!"

"That's precisely why we need your help—"

"Forget it. It's not going to happen."

"That's no good," Tess replied quietly.

"But it's the way it is."

For a few moments they glared at each other in silence.

Suddenly an engine pulsed ominously in the sky. They looked up and could just make out a surveillance drone flying overhead through the mist.

"Police patrol," Herzog said. "They're always flying over. You should be careful."

"Why?" Tess said. "We're not the ones hiding things."

Herzog really didn't like her. "Cillian, if you're smart, you'll stop now. All you'll find inside Gilgamesh is pain. Go back to your life, forget this happened, and in future ..." Herzog glanced warily at Tess, "... choose your friends more carefully."

He turned and walked back down the path, leaving them standing by the grave.

# 35

Tess checked her smartCell and found a Standard Design Roadhouse just a few kilometres away.

With 24/7 stores, recharge points for vehicles, a choice of diners and some overnight rooms, the SDRs had spread like a rash across the Provinces, replacing village shops and pubs with merciless efficiency. Clean, characterless and functional, it was the perfect place to crash while working out their next move.

Cillian slumped on the bed and closed his eyes. For a few blissful moments his mind flashed back to the WallScreen in his study-pod covered with equations. He longed for the security of that world now. Numbers could be controlled and manipulated; they had certainty and logic, unlike the real world where everything was a hopeless tangle of half-truths.

"Maybe Natasha's grave explains the missing 3 years," Tess suggested.

Cillian opened his eyes, reluctantly facing reality again.

"Whoever your mother was, for some reason she had to be written out of the picture."

"Why was Herzog so suspicious of you?"

Tess felt the full force of Cillian's gaze. "Don't get hung up on that. He was trying to divide us. I doubt he even told us half of what he knows."

But still Cillian looked at her, unblinking. "Do you think my father was being paid off? For something he did in Gilgamesh, something terrible?"

"It's possible."

"It would explain why Herzog fell out with him."

"Herzog falls out with everyone. He's that type."

"But what if he's right? Maybe we should stop now before we find things we wish we hadn't."

"Your father *wanted* you to know," Tess urged. "That's why he told you about Gilgamesh. He wanted you to do this. If you don't confront it, you'll be haunted by it your whole life."

Cillian rolled onto his side. "I'm not so sure."

"Those people who broke into your apartment, do you think *they'll* stop? You can't walk away from this because they won't."

She reached out and turned his face back towards her. "We need to get into Gilgamesh. We need to find out what's really going on in there."

"Herzog said it's impossible—"

"Do you trust me?"

"Should I?"

Tess smiled. "Good answer."

But Cillian hadn't meant it as a joke.

"Let me make a few calls," Tess said.

"To who?"

"Just let me do what I'm good at. You should get some

rest." She brushed Cillian's eyelids closed with her fingers and rested her hand gently on his forehead. "I'll sort everything."

There were so many conflicting patterns in Cillian's mind, it was exhausting trying to hold it together. He had lost all fixed points, which made it impossible to know who to believe. Right now the only comfort was Tess's cool hand on his head. Maybe she was right. Maybe if he could just rest for a while, everything would start to resolve...

Tess watched quietly as Cillian's breathing became slow and steady, then in one eerie moment, all the muscles in his body seemed to lose their tension ... and he was in a deep sleep.

Quietly Tess went into the bathroom, closed the door and entered the security codes on her smartCell to contact Revelation.

Stored messages from Blackwood scrolled across her screen: *Checking you're safe. Confirm ... Do you want me to prep an extraction team? ... Comms check. Please verify ... Tess, are you OK*? He'd been pinging her every couple of hours.

Tess knew she'd broken protocol by not replying. In fast-moving situations Blackwood liked to keep a close eye on his operatives, but this was the first chance she'd had to respond.

She started to type, then hesitated.

Tess opened the bathroom door and looked at Cillian sleeping on the bed. He seemed so isolated and vulnerable.

She swiped her smartCell and shut the messaging app down. No need to contact Revelation, not just yet. Right now everyone wanted the same thing. Cillian needed answers and Revelation needed answers. Beyond that...

No need to think beyond that.

Not just yet.

# 36

Silently Tess left the bedroom and went downstairs to the diner. A couple of people were sitting at the bar, but they weren't paying attention to anything except the burbling WallScreen. On the far side of the room was a line of booths like the payphones you saw in old movies.

Tess picked the corner one, out of sight of the bar, and locked the door behind her. The interactive display sparked to life. *"The world at your fingertips,"* it chirped. *"You want it, we print it!"*

Tess hit *Mute*.

The booth flipped to visual menus, scrolling through options, but Tess had other ideas.

All printed goods were logged for tax and to prevent illegal downloads, so she typed a line of hack code into the search bar and a few moments later was into the operating system. Placing her smartCell screen-to-screen with the printer, she uploaded the masking software and slipped onto the Darknet.

Now she could work without being traced.

She went straight to the Revelation servers and logged on to the weapons database, a formidable virtual armoury with everything for the assassin on the move – hunting knives, motor-driven garrottes, wrist blades, retractable batons.

And guns.

Dozens of guns.

She flicked through the menus, searching for the Doc Holliday, an assault pistol with burst capability that was small enough to be hidden under clothing and could be burnt after use.

Tess double-clicked to download. Seconds later a box under the screen lit up and the printer whirred into action. Grimly she watched the arms dance back and forth, spraying polymers with micro-precision, building the gun layer by layer. The sweet candyfloss smell of molten plastic filled the booth. It was so unlike the smell of death.

# 37

Herzog woke with a start to find the barrel of a gun pressed hard into his temple.

"Do exactly as I say, or I'll kill you," Tess said coldly.

"For God's sake—"

"Last warning."

"OK, OK." Herzog glanced at her finger poised on the trigger as if it was the most natural thing in the world. "You're Revelation, aren't you?" He rubbed his hands over his face, trying to think clearly. "They warned us. They said someone like you would be coming. Sooner or later."

"Because P8 is wrong. And you know it."

"It's not that simple."

"You *know* it!"

"It was different in the beginning. But they went further..."

"And you never had the guts to do anything about it."

"You can't just press the stop button."

"But you didn't even try!"

"Please, it's not my battle."

"That is *exactly* where you've failed," Tess said with conviction. "If something is wrong, you have to act."

"I'm just trying to get by—"

"You did *nothing*. That's a sin. And sin gets punished."

"I don't deserve this. Please ... I'm just a tiny part of it."

Tess despised Herzog's cowardice, but she knew better than to make this personal. "I'm going to give you one chance to atone. Atone and you can live."

"What about Cillian?" Herzog asked.

"Worry about yourself."

"What'll happen to him?"

Tess hesitated.

"He's one of them, isn't he?"

"He's the most important lead we have," Tess said evasively. "We can help him find out what he needs to know."

"And when he gets the answers? What then?"

"Where is the weakness in P8's security?"

"There isn't a weakness."

"Think!" She lashed out, cracking the pistol across his head.

"You can't get in—"

She grabbed him and forced him to the ground. "We can. And we will."

Herzog looked up into the barrel of the gun. He could see that this girl had been trained by killers.

"You've got 3 seconds," Tess said, her finger tightening on the trigger.

"You'll never get past security. There are cameras, body scanners—"

"What about the building works? The forest comes

right up to the perimeter fence. Can we get in that way?"

Herzog's hesitation was the only answer Tess needed. "So it *can* be done," she said. "And when we've crossed the grounds, there's a way into the building, isn't there?"

No reply.

"*Isn't there?*"

"Yes."

"But we'll need a security pass and codes. Which you have—"

"You won't get more than 100 metres—"

"And which you're going to give me."

No reply.

Tess jammed the gun into his forehead. "One way or another, I'll get what I need."

"All right." Herzog nodded weakly.

He got to his feet, went to a small safe under the desk and typed in the combination. But as he took out the security pass, he felt a sharp pinprick in his neck. Herzog spun round to see Tess clutching a hypodermic needle.

"You bitch! I've given you everything!" he said, furiously clawing at his neck.

"It won't kill you," Tess said calmly. "But when you wake up, we'll be long gone."

Herzog felt the strength drain from his body as he slumped to his knees. He saw Tess lean over him, felt her breath on the side of his face as she spoke:

"If you raise the alarm, if you try to act against me, if you even tell anyone I was here, Revelation will find you. And kill you."

They were the last words Herzog heard before he blacked out.

# 38

"How the hell did you get it?"

"Herzog had a change of heart." Tess handed him the security pass. "Turns out he wants to help after all."

Cillian looked uneasily at the chip-enabled card. "What did you do to him, Tess?"

"Don't start panicking."

"I'm not panicking!"

"Good. Because I sorted this as well." She tossed the gun onto the bed.

"Are you serious?"

"We're off the map now. We have to watch our backs."

Cillian picked up the gun and studied it apprehensively. The smell of the polymers was still fresh.

"Life out here is cheaper." Tess shrugged.

"Do you even know how to use it?"

"Please. I told you I had a difficult childhood."

For a few moments Cillian said nothing; this girl obviously had connections to some very dark places. "Who are you really?" he asked softly, almost dreading the answer. "Who do you work for?"

"Like I told you, I fight for myself. I always have."

But Cillian knew there was more to it than that. He handed the gun back. "I'm sorry."

"I thought you wanted the truth?"

"Not if it's soaked in blood."

"Life isn't some maths problem to be sorted out on a screen."

"I didn't sign up for this."

"In the real world things get rough!"

"So we just throw morality out of the window?"

"Morality is *exactly* what we're fighting for. You and I. Right now." She brandished the gun. "With this."

"I'm not a terrorist. There's got to be a better way."

Tess sat down next to him, close, so that he could feel the warmth of her body. "You know, there was a remote tribe in Assam Province that didn't believe in violence. They wanted to live in peace and harmony with the whole world. Then one night, a tiger came out of the jungle and ate them all."

"And?"

"And nothing. End of story."

Cillian looked at her, and couldn't help a grim smile. "Is that really true?"

"It's true every day, in a hundred different ways." Gently Tess put the gun back in his hands. "What you *should* be asking is why didn't I get one for you as well?"

# 39

2 hours later, as dawn broke across the freezing sky, Cillian and Tess were perched in the tree canopy a few metres back from the top of an electrified fence. From here they could see the whole north side of the Gilgamesh complex.

"They're certainly in a hurry to get it built," Cillian said, looking at the army of workmen who had been toiling through the night. "Whatever it is…"

The grounds rolled down to the cliff edge where they met the dark ocean swell, but in the middle of the space a massive sinkhole had been bored deep into the rock. From this angle it was impossible to see how far down the chasm stretched, but the cranes clustered around the lip seemed to take for ever lowering girders and cable drums into the floodlit depths.

"I think they're nearly ready," Tess said. She was pointing further along the perimeter fence to where a section was about to be removed so that a tunnelling machine could trundle on-site. It meant the power to the electric fence would be cut for a while.

Suddenly Cillian felt a change in the air. "That's it," he said. "It's off."

Tess looked at him sceptically. "How can you be so sure?"

"Can't you feel it?" Cillian dropped down from the tree.

"Be careful," she warned.

He strode towards the fence, reached out, grabbed the wire – and suddenly his whole body spasmed violently.

"Cillian!" She leapt down and ran towards the fence, but he was already laughing.

"Just kidding."

"Don't!" She whacked him.

Cillian clambered up the mesh, slid between the barbed wire at the top and dropped down on the other side. "Easy."

"Not bad for a university boy." Tess followed him over, and quickly they made their way to a cluster of temporary cabins 100 metres away. Lights were burning in the first one where foremen were poring over plans. Beyond that were some equipment cabins.

After a few attempts, they found one stacked with safety helmets and high-vis jackets. When they emerged, Cillian and Tess looked like a couple of workers starting their shift.

"Hitch up that trailer. The one with the drainage pipes," Tess said, as she climbed onto a construction quad bike. "As long as we look busy, no-one'll ask questions."

A few minutes later, theirs was just one of dozens of vehicles churning up the slushy mud around the gaping mouth of the sinkhole.

They followed one of the main tracks to get closer to the old buildings, then veered off and headed down to the boiler rooms built into the lowest level of the Gothic fortress.

When they were out of sight of the main works, Tess slowed the quad and gazed up at the sheer granite walls. "Looks more like a prison than a hospital."

"I think that's our best hope for getting in," Cillian said, pointing to some service doors leading off the yard.

"Let's spin the quad around. We might need a fast getaway."

As they walked towards the buildings, a set of doors burst open, startling them, but it was only a group of kitchen porters hauling boxes of food on pallets.

"All right?" Tess smiled. "Just got to tap into the main feeds."

"Sure." The disinterested porters nodded and held the doors open, allowing them both inside.

"What feeds?" Cillian whispered as they hurried away.

"I don't know. But nor did they."

They made their way deeper into the kitchen complex, past stores and prep areas and rooms that seemed to have been forgotten altogether, until finally they came up against a formidable steel security door. Beyond it was the old heart of Gilgamesh.

*Restricted Access.*

They hid their high-vis jackets behind some shelving, then Tess took out the stolen security pass and swiped it across the sensor.

Nothing happened.

Had Herzog somehow raised the alarm? Had he cancelled his pass? Were they walking into a trap?

"Do it slower," Cillian suggested.

She tried again. There was a beep, then a prompt asked for the access code.

"I knew that," Tess said, typing in the code.

Bolts clunked back, there was a breath of compressed air...

Cillian and Tess braced themselves.

But as the door opened they were engulfed by a wave of heat and the strangely reassuring smell of clean laundry.

# 40

It was a different world on this side of the security doors. There was no trace of forbidding grey granite; in here everything was bright and polished and high-tech. The white walls were infused with information screens and a soft light emanated from the smooth floor. The sense of peace was overwhelming.

They heard a whirring approach along the gently curving corridor and instinctively pulled back into an alcove. But as the sound came closer, Tess relaxed. "I know that whirr."

She peered around the corner and saw a Maintenance-Bot diligently polishing the floor. It was the same brand as those that lived on the SkyWay – same servos, same whirr. "Nothing to worry about from him."

Cillian took the security pass, swiped it across a display screen and pulled up an interactive diagram mapping the labyrinth of old buildings.

The scale of the complex was overwhelming. The

Gothic castle was just a shell that covered a vast network of laboratories and wards; some tunnelled deep into the ground, 10 levels down, others stretched up, boring right through the centre of the old buildings.

"Where the hell do we begin?" Tess said, paging through map after map, but Cillian's eyes had already locked onto the ward halls. He zoomed in on a series of concentric circles with ominous labels—

*Bestiary*

*Glass-Cribs*

*Speculative*

*Sub-Prime*

*High-Grade*

The names betrayed a ruthless logic to whatever was being done in Gilgamesh.

"Let's start there," Cillian said apprehensively, touching the closest ward hall on the display: *Sub-Prime.*

"We're not going to get far just walking around," Tess said.

"Maybe there's a way through the service corridors." Cillian searched the map for the most obscure route, and noticed an area labelled *Maintenance-Bots: Charging.*

"How about that?"

Tess immediately understood. "Perfect. No-one looks twice at a broken bot."

10 minutes later they wheeled a de-powered Cleaning-Bot into the Sub-Prime ward as if doing a routine replacement. None of the medical staff even glanced at them.

Cillian looked up into the hall. It was a massive circular cavern with a ramp spiralling up the outside wall to a domed skylight at the top. But there were no beds here. There were cells. Countless individual cells lining the entire length of the ramp, like a high-tech prison.

As they started to wheel the bot up the slope they realized that each cell contained only one patient, and all the rooms were glass-fronted, giving medical staff the power of total observation 24/7. BioDisplays scrolled on the glass walls, relaying information from a battery of instruments inside, and a host of cameras deprived the patients of any last shred of privacy.

The first cell they passed contained a teenage girl, gazing at a WallScreen that played high-speed images of clouds tumbling across a mountain range.

Her skin was hanging half-off.

Not from a wound, but because she was shedding it like a snake. The old skin hung around her waist, revealing a new one glistening down her back.

As they approached, the girl flicked her head around, locking eyes with Cillian.

For a moment he faltered under her intense gaze.

"Don't stop," Tess whispered urgently.

Cillian forced himself to look away. "Who's done this to them?"

"Just keep moving."

Fearfully they continued up the ramp, past some more skin-shedders, until they came to a boy who could have been no more than 12, prowling around his cell on all fours. Not on hands and feet, but on 4 identical limbs that were neither arms nor legs, but something in between. Something new.

As if sensing their approach, the boy suddenly stopped and raised his head, staring intently. Cillian flinched and turned away, but he could still feel the boy's unrelenting eyes on him.

They passed more "Posture Cells" containing young

children. Some could only crawl, others had to slither across the floor as if they'd been cursed.

"They're kids!" It made Cillian feel sick. "They're just kids."

"I think these may be the lucky ones," Tess said ominously. She looked over the glass balustrade down into the lobby, where medical staff clustered around a monitoring hub. Doctors were quietly talking as they studied screens and flipped between displays, but Tess knew this wasn't about nursing. No-one was being healed here, they were being studied like specimens in a bell jar.

A clattering sound drew Cillian further up the ramp to a large cell criss-crossed with bars. Several children, no older than 7, were leaping around the frames with incredible ease, like free runners let loose in a zoo. Even though their physical prowess was extraordinary and their reactions razor-sharp, they seemed to have the minds of animals, and could only shriek and yell to communicate with each other.

And yet even they fell silent and huddled together, staring at Cillian with unblinking eyes as he approached.

With every cell they passed, new horrors unfolded. There were children with no mouths or noses, but with gill-like slits in their bodies for breathing. Whoever had done this to them had been experimenting with different configurations. One child had a row of slits in his neck, another all down her back.

As Cillian and Tess walked past, the children rolled into tanks of water that dominated their cells and stared out from the safety of underwater, slowly breathing through their gills.

Further up the ramp led to fresh abominations. A teenager alone in a cell with skin so translucent you could see the blood pumping in her veins and her sinews tensing. She stood by the far wall, compulsively drawing with an electronic stylus, covering the white space with intricate patterns.

Another teenager in the adjacent cell had the same paper-thin skin, but he was covering his walls with numbers; not randomly, but in a calculation, a massive calculation.

Cillian was immediately drawn into the numbers, his mind hunting for patterns, trying to follow the game. Suddenly he got it. The boy was creating a complex 3-dimensional maze-solving algorithm.

"Beautiful," Cillian whispered.

The boy turned his head and a smile flickered across his face, as if this stranger was the first person who had really understood what he was doing. But in the next instant the boy's smile vanished and he curled up, wrapping his arms across his body, suddenly ashamed of his own naked transparency.

Cillian closed his eyes and leant forward, resting his head on the glass wall. Tess could see he was unsteady, as if he was about to faint. She grabbed his arm and pulled him through some doors that led to a medical supplies bay. "Pitying them won't help. Stay focussed."

But Cillian was overwhelmed. He reached out to a WallScreen and gazed in horror at the gently glowing map. "If that's a ward ... what happens there?" He pointed to even more ominous areas—

*Non-Viable*

*Psychosis*

*Maladapted*

Suddenly a set of warning lights started blinking on the map.

"That's not good." Tess opened the door and peered back down the ramp. Nurses were running from cell to cell. Something seemed to be wrong with the patients.

And then Tess realized – all of them were staring up the ramp, their eyes searching for Cillian.

The nurses looked up, following the patients' gaze, and Tess flung herself back against the wall.

"We have to get out of here!"

# 41

Tess kicked the Maintenance-Bot hard and watched it pick up speed, hurtling down the spiral ramp towards the nurses, who yelled for help.

An alarm started sounding—

Medics shouted over each other. *"Lock down the ward!" "Keep the patients safe!"*

But as the Cleaning-Bot ricocheted like a lethal pinball, cracking glass walls and shorting out the BioDisplays, it spread fear and panic from cell to cell. Already patients were throwing themselves against the floor, seized by hysteria.

*"Use sedation!"*

*"Don't let them self-harm!"*

Grimly Tess looked down at the disarray. "We've got about 30 seconds!" she shouted to Cillian.

As they bolted up the ramp, Tess unholstered her gun and fired a burst of bullets into the glass dome that arched over the ward hall. There was an ominous groan as cracks grew like frost, then with a massive punch the entire glass curve shattered.

Cillian watched, mesmerized, as glass rained down into the chasm, lacerating the hands of the medics who tried to protect their faces. Spatters of red appeared like paint-bursts on the white floor—

Blood sprayed over pristine monitoring stations—

For a few harrowing moments Cillian was plunged back into the Metro crash; the chaos of death—

"MOVE!" Tess's voice snapped him forwards again. She gripped his arm and hauled him up the ramp towards the gaping hole where the dome used to be.

She stopped at the last cell and aimed her gun at a patient cowering behind the glass wall.

"NO!" Sick with horror, Cillian tried to grab the weapon but Tess pulled away.

"Stand back!" she yelled at the patient. "BACK!"

She fired into the wall which shattered, punching glass fragments all around the screaming patient.

"It's all right! I'm not going to hurt you!"

But the patient scrambled into a corner in terror, hands clamped over his head.

"What are you doing?" Cillian yelled.

Tess ignored him and stepped into the cell. "I'm not going to hurt you! I promise," she said to the patient who was now frenzied with fear. It was the portable control panel she was after – a mobile console linked to the main system by a long loom of cable. Ripping the plugs out, she grabbed the cable, dragged it from the cell and thrust it at Cillian.

"Throw it up there." She pointed to all that remained of the dome – a curved steel girder 10 metres above them. "DO IT!"

Cillian wound the cable around his arm like a lasso, looked up at the girder ... and paused as energy permeated his body like a wash of warmth.

Suddenly everything felt easy, his arms understood what needed to be done. He threw the coil of rope-wire ... watched it ripple through the air ... bounce off the girder ... and flip over.

Tess grabbed the loose end, tied it off around the handrail and swung out into the void, slithering up the wires. At the top she grabbed the girder and hauled herself outside.

Cillian gripped the cables and followed her up, hand over hand. But halfway something made him pause. He looked down into the space plunging away beneath his feet and felt a rush of exhilaration; a moment of pure freedom, suspended in the void, the strength in his own arms the only thing holding him here.

"Hurry!" Tess shouted down.

Cillian's hands moved again, hauling himself onto the roof where Tess was pacing the parapet, looking for the best way down.

"Their security is all about stopping people getting *in*," she said. "They're not so used to dealing with people getting *out*."

She peered over the edge of the building. On one side was a sheer drop into the rock-strewn ocean, but on the other side the wall intersected a series of sloping roofs that terraced back to ground level.

"That's the way," she said, pointing down the vertical wall. "The granite blocks should give us finger grips."

Cillian peered over the side of the building into the precipitous drop, and for a few seconds was seized by the urge to jump. He felt so empowered, as if nothing could harm him.

Slowly he leant out…

"Cillian!" She grabbed him as if realizing what he was thinking. "Be careful."

"It's OK." He crouched down and swung his legs over the edge until they found the first crack in the stones.

*I see it.*

In an instant he glimpsed a pattern of larger gaps between the granite blocks and knew which was the least treacherous route down.

Tess watched him climb, hardly able to believe how easy he made it look. She swung out and tried to follow his path – same toeholds and ledges, but every move was painful, the freezing granite cut into her fingers and her feet slipped on the damp walls.

When they were a few metres from the lower roof, Cillian let go of the wall and dropped, rolling down the slate tiles to the next level.

"How hard can it be?" Tess muttered to herself, and let go as well.

A moment of free fall—

Then she smashed into the roof and slid down, out of control, leaving a jagged spray of broken tiles in her wake.

As the end of the roof rushed closer, she reached out to try to grab the gutter, but she was going too fast and overshot…

THUMP! Onto the next roof down.

Half-falling, half-scrambling, Tess finally managed to slow herself just enough to make the final leap into the service yards.

Cillian helped her to her feet. "You all right?"

She looked up at the sheer walls, amazed that she was still alive. "Let's hope that was the hardest part."

They ran around the base of the building towards the quad bike. Tess fired it up and gunned the engine; as Cillian sat behind her she opened the throttle and roared across the grounds—

When suddenly an ugly rising wail echoed off all the buildings. The General Alarm.

"Too late to worry about that now." Tess accelerated hard, heading straight for the gap in the fence where the workmen were still wrangling wire.

"We'll have to find another way!"

"They'll move!" she shouted back.

Tess saw the foreman try to marshal his men into a cordon, but they just ran for cover.

Furious, the foreman leapt into a bulldozer and started to position it across the gap himself.

Tess twisted the throttle wide open, making the quad bike bounce violently across the uneven ground, forcing Cillian to tighten his grip around her waist.

The bulldozer roared, its tracks churning up mud—

Tess closed her eyes and prayed—

The gap grew smaller and smaller—

As the quad hurtled through, its rear wheel clipped the 'dozer's front blade and it twisted round.

Still Tess refused to let go of the throttle.

The bike did a massive wheelspin as it landed, sending up a curtain of mud, then she jammed the steering left and headed for the cover of the trees.

Finally they were away.

Outside Gilgamesh.

Only now they were prey.

# 42

The densely packed trees forced Tess to slow the quad down. There was no easy way through the forest, no path to follow, just a tangle of snow-covered branches.

"How much fuel have we got?" Cillian peered over her shoulder to see the readout.

But Tess had already clocked an ominous engine sound approaching fast from above. "I don't think fuel's the problem."

Seconds later a helicopter roared low over the tree canopy, its powerful searchlight hunting through the forest.

Instinctively Tess veered away from the beam of light, but that just pushed them into denser forest which slowed them even more. Every time she tried to open the throttle, low-hanging branches snapped viciously at them, trying to pull them off the quad; but when she eased back, the implacable searchlight swept closer.

As the trap tightened, Cillian's senses started to over-process.

*I see it.*

A way through the complex mesh of trees.

Moments later he felt that strange sense of empower-
ment flood through him, urging him to surrender to his
reflexes. His body was screaming that it knew how to survive this, how to tap into primal skills to elude a predator.

*It knew.*

He stretched his arms past Tess and gripped the han-
dlebars. "Let go."

"What do you mean?"

"I can do this."

"No!"

"Trust me," he said.

Tess heard the eerie calm in his voice, then she
seemed to feel the energy around him shift. Praying it
was the right call, she took her hands off the grips.

Cillian jammed open the throttle, his body reacted
and his whole world slowed to a beautiful tranquility.
They were gliding slowly, softly through the forest like
ghosts. The numbers on the speedo were shooting up,
but his own mind was now revving so fast it became
effortless to find a path through the tight forest.

For Tess it was a terrifying, chaotic blur of branches
as the quad lurched violently from side to side. No-one
could drive this fast without killing themselves.

*No-one.*

She closed her eyes and waited for the devastating
crash and searing pain that would destroy them—

When suddenly the brakes slammed on.

She opened her eyes. By some miracle they were out
of the woods. Tess looked back. The helicopter was way
behind them, still searching above the trees. They had
outrun it.

"You may want to close your eyes again," Cillian suggested, as he veered the quad to the right and over the crest of a snow bank. Below them was a terrifyingly steep slope leading down to the valley.

"No!" It wasn't just the angle of the drop, it was the swathes of ice that zigzagged across it.

"We've got to get away."

"Not down there!"

"There's no choice."

"It *can't* be done!"

"I think the trick is not to brake." And with a roar of the engine, Cillian plunged the quad over the edge.

Tess barely breathed as they careened downwards, skidding wildly across the ice, veering past jagged boulders.

But Cillian had never felt more in control. His instincts were calculating every move and swerve with unnerving accuracy. It was like having a sixth sense that could read momentum and gravity and friction without thinking.

*Without thinking.*

As the quad finally roared off the side of the mountain and into the snow-covered valley, Tess was overwhelmed with nausea from the adrenaline rush.

She knew what they'd just done was impossible for any normal human being; and that proved beyond doubt what Cillian really was.

But she also knew that no normal human being could have just saved her life like that.

# 43

Moving low and fast across the snowy landscape, surrounded by nothing but mountains and the biting cold, they could have been running with the wolves. It was only the roar of the engine that kept it real.

Tess glanced over her shoulder at the wooded ridge far behind. The helicopter was still sweeping the trees with its spotlight, outwitted for now, but she knew it wouldn't be long before they broadened the search area. She glanced at the long, straight tracks the quad was leaving in its wake. Even though the wind was blowing the snow smooth, their tyre tracks were still visible.

"We need to head lower," she shouted to Cillian. "Out of the snowfield."

"OK. Whatever you think."

She took control and steered the quad bike towards a wide gulley where several streams converged, but after a few minutes the snow gave way to marshy ground and every jolt sent the chunky wheels plunging deeper into cloying wet ruts. Tess gunned the engine to keep going, spraying them both with rank mud, but the ground became softer and softer.

"We're going to get swallowed up!" Cillian shouted over the revving engine.

But Tess kept the quad slithering through the mud until they reached one of the streams winding across the marsh, then she jumped it down into the icy water. Immediately the wheels hit the pebbly bed they got traction, and roared off again. "Just because you did the trees doesn't mean you know everything!" she called back.

"I never doubted you."

"Right."

They powered along the stream, trying to ignore the bitterly cold water that soaked them. Cillian held Tess tightly to preserve the warmth of their bodies, but the further they went the deeper the cold cut in, until even the warmth of the quad's engine started to fail. The more it whined, the harder Tess pushed it, willing it to keep going.

2 agonizing kilometres later, they saw the lights and steam-stacks of a vast, sprawling industrial plant in the distance.

"Looks like a BoilDown," Cillian said.

Tess brought the quad to a stop. "We should hole up there. Try and get warm."

Neither of them had ever actually been to a BoilDown, but all school kids learnt about them – vast recycling centres in the middle of nowhere which broke down the millions of tons of junk and unwanted stuff that poured out of Foundation City. With just a skeleton crew controlling the massive, lumbering machines that ate through twisted mountains of debris, a BoilDown was the perfect place to hide.

By the time they reached the outer garbage field, the quad was on its last legs, sputtering painfully like an exhausted beast. Cillian and Tess rolled it next to a pyramid of assorted mechanical junk, gave it an appreciative pat on the fuel tank, then headed deeper into the trash.

"This is really weird," Cillian whispered as they wandered through huge avenues of unwanted goods.

Plumes of smoke rose from the TechnoSmelters, where robot parts and circuit boards were boiled and their precious elements skimmed off. Satellite-controlled diggers shaped and reshaped the landscape of trash to make sure the smelters never went hungry, and the whole thing was powered by an array of vast wind turbines whose blades chopped the air with a menacing thud.

"How about over there?" Cillian pointed to a labyrinth that had been built out of LCD screens patiently waiting for destruction.

Tess nodded. "At least it'll be out of the wind."

As they made their way across, she studied the sky and saw a cluster of dots on the far horizon, hovering over the marshland they'd just crossed. "Surveillance drones. They'll be searching with infrared."

Cillian looked at the plumes of smoke billowing from the TechnoSmelters. "Will the heat from them mask us?"

"I hope so."

"You really think we'll be safe?"

"We're a long way from safe," Tess said quietly. "But at least here we can wait for the drones to give up."

She led the way into the LCD shelter and slumped down. Cillian sat next to her.

"You OK?" she asked. "Apart from exhausted, cold and hungry."

He nodded, but said nothing.

Then Tess watched as Cillian put his hands over his face, and vanished deep into his own thoughts.

# 44

The evidence from Gilgamesh rolled across a WallScreen 1,200 kilometres away: CCTV images, entry and exit points, aerial footage of the hostile terrain across which the quad bike had escaped.

"Were any of the subjects harmed?" Gabrielle asked when Cole had finished his briefing.

"Fortunately not."

"I mean the whole point of running trials out there is to keep them safe from this kind of attack."

"I don't think it was an attack," Paige interjected. "Not this time."

"She was armed," Cole said irritably. "She fired in anger."

"But she made a point of *not* killing any of the patients."

Gabrielle walked over to the screen and studied the frozen image of Cillian. "It's incredible, isn't it? Last week he was just a student with a head for numbers. Now look what he can do. Put him in a struggle for survival, a real struggle, and the things we engineered into him are self-activating."

"The problem is he's not alone." Cole pulled up a picture of the quad bike speeding towards the security fence. "Now he's tangled up with Revelation."

"Which means he's in real danger," Paige added.

"From *her*?" Gabrielle enlarged the image. Tess was driving, Cillian sat behind, arms around her waist. "I don't think so."

"That's not the point," Cole insisted. "That girl is witnessing everything."

"But that's what's so interesting. It's *because* of the danger the girl's putting him in that he's triggering."

"And at any moment she could turn round and kill him," Paige said bluntly.

"Come on." Gabrielle waved her hand dismissively. "I thought we had more guts than this."

"We're gambling with his life."

"I know what you're saying. But what's happening here is incredible." Gabrielle's eyes were fired with excitement. "Cillian's father died. He was lost and disorientated. The world he knew was crumbling, and his *body* reacted. His instincts changed, without us doing anything, no drugs, no intervention, nothing." She looked at Cole and Paige. "It's a testament to the quality of your work that he's so far ahead. You should be proud."

"But what if the pressure makes him unstable?" Paige asked. "What if he's spinning out of control?"

"Why do you doubt his resilience?"

"Because it's untested."

"It's the pressure that's making him come alive," Gabrielle said. "Conflict, the struggle with death, grappling with the unknown ... that's what drives us all, isn't it?"

"So we just watch him suffer?"

"You're getting too emotional about this whole thing. He's not suffering. He's searching. For answers."

"I think he's searching for *you*." Paige looked at Gabrielle, trying to connect to the woman rather than the scientist.

"Maybe ... but that's quite a leap."

"And if we don't help him, then the experiment just got cruel."

"You sound like one of those people who don't like seeing death in nature documentaries."

"He's not an animal—"

"Of course he is!" Gabrielle saw how annoyed Paige was at the rebuke and checked herself. "I'm sorry, I didn't mean it like that."

Paige shrugged, but said nothing.

"I just don't want us to forget how valuable Cillian is," Gabrielle went on. "He's the first of the Line to start questioning his own identity, to ask 'Who am I?' I want to know how he's going to answer that. I really do."

"Please, let's just bring him in," Paige tried one last time. "For his own safety."

"We can't do that." Gabrielle was adamant. "We need to let this run as long as we can."

"So what are we going to do about Revelation?" Cole asked. "Are we just going to ignore the threat?"

"Of course not. Cillian needs our protection, but not our interference. Brief security. They can set up an extraction plan."

It was only after Cole and Paige had left that Gabrielle

allowed doubt to creep back into her thoughts.

She gazed at the images of Cillian scrolling on the WallScreen. She knew everything about him as a biological entity: the unique balance of his hormones, every letter of his DNA, the intricate biochemistry of his flesh and blood. But as a person...

Her fingers touched the pixels that were his face, trying to read his expression. Should she stand back and watch? Or reach out and help?

That he might be searching for her gave Gabrielle a strange flutter of vulnerability. Was Paige right? Was it cruel to leave him out there?

Suddenly she reached out and hit the keypad, wiping the images from the screen.

Keep it professional.

Stay focussed.

The last thing Gabrielle needed was emotion clouding her logic. This was just an experiment, no different to the thousands of others that had defined her life.

# 45

Tess could only watch as Cillian sank deeper and deeper into himself.

Several times she tried to talk to him, but he didn't even look up; he just remained slumped on the ground as if his overloaded mind had shut down to protect itself. It was unnerving to be with someone who was so frighteningly absent.

As dawn broke, Tess heard the sound of the drones' engines retreating. "I was beginning to think they'd never give up." She peered through a gap in the trash, trying to glimpse the sky. "Half an hour and we can make a move."

Finally, slowly, Cillian lifted his head. "I'm ready now," he said quietly.

"Are you all right?"

No reply.

"I've got to say, Cillian, you were pretty awesome back there," she said, trying to sound casual. "We were lucky to escape."

"I didn't escape." Cillian looked at her with deeply troubled eyes. "I may be out here, but I can never escape. I see that now. Those faces in the glass cells ... you saw how they looked at me. At *me*. Not you. They recognized me. As one of their own."

Tess went very still, desperate not to give anything away with the slightest wrong reaction.

"In here." Cillian touched his forehead. "That's where it started. I used to think it was just about numbers and patterns, but the truth is, something happens ... it's like I'm being taken over from the inside ... physically. Somehow I can move through time more slowly. It's the only reason I survived the Metro bomb. It's how we got through the forest and across the snowfield. Deep down, my mind has been ... deformed. Twisted out of shape." He closed his eyes, struggling to admit the worst. "And I think it was my father who did it. He was involved in those experiments. It's why I'm like this."

As Tess looked at him, Cillian's strangeness seemed to melt away, leaving behind a boy trapped in his own terrible isolation.

"You don't know that for sure, Cillian."

"It's the only thing that makes sense. I'm not a son, I never was. I'm just an experiment."

"That's not true. You can't just tear up years of memories. Your father loved you—"

"Did he?"

"You had a life together. He nurtured you, protected you. You're not locked away somewhere—"

"For how much longer? Maybe now he's dead they're going to take me back. Maybe that's what this is all about."

"Then we have to stay one step ahead."

"No." Cillian stood up defiantly. "I'm not running any more."

"We need to stay calm and think this through—"

"I'm done with thinking! I'm going back to the City. I'm going to blow this wide open. Gilgamesh, P8, everything we've seen, all over the Ultranet. People need to know what's really going on."

"You think they'll believe you?"

"I don't care what they do to me. They're experimenting on human beings! On children."

"I thought you were smarter than this," Tess said, desperately trying to pull him back under control.

"And I thought *you* were the one who wanted to fight. To expose the truth."

"When the time is right."

"We've seen how wrong this is. With our own eyes. What more do you need, Tess?" He turned and walked out into the open. "What more do you need?"

She let him go, let him have some space. Tess knew she had to play this very carefully, because if she lost Cillian's trust he would be of no further use to Revelation.

And that was a very dangerous place to be.

# 46

At the Northern Hub, Cillian and Tess ran straight into a wall of security checks. They may have had train tickets, but their clothes were trashed and their hands suspiciously cut and bruised. Tess's big fear was that Gilgamesh had already circulated CCTV images and arrest warrants to the police.

Doggedly she and Cillian stuck to their cover story, that they were hikers who'd got caught in a flash flood, and eventually they were let inside.

Despite everything, it felt good to be back in a cocoon of civilization. Warmth and comfort reflected off every glossy surface. People were chatting over coffee, kids laughed as they ran around the gaming cloisters. Everything was reassuringly normal.

Cillian checked the schedule for the Bullet Train that would whisk them back to Foundation City. They had just over an hour to sort themselves out. After buying new clothes in the mall, they hired a couple of washroom suites to get cleaned and dressed.

Tess turned her steam-shower cubicle on to full blast, and while it warmed up she piggy-backed her smartCell onto the Hub's system. Second attempt she got into Revelation's network, and immediately started uploading her video footage. For the entire time they'd been in Gilgamesh, Tess had been covertly filming: maps of the complex, the layout of the ward halls, the strange mutated children imprisoned in *Sub-Prime*.

As she watched the upload bar flick across the screen, she could imagine the effect this was having at Cotton Wharf. It was the first time Revelation had penetrated so deeply into the workings of P8.

Moments after the last video went through, her smartCell rang. It was Blackwood. "Tess, are you safe?"

"Did you see it?"

"I know. It's incredible."

"There's *nothing* incredible about it."

"I didn't mean—"

"You weren't there! You didn't see their pain."

"Theirs and who knows how many others," Blackwood insisted. "That's why we're fighting."

"How long are you going to let P8 get away with this?"

"No-one's getting away with anything. I promise."

"All those victims—"

"Need *you* to be strong, Tess. In one day you've pushed Revelation forward years. Everything we've feared, you've proved is true. *You've* done that – I can't tell you how proud I am."

Tess nodded, but said nothing. Pride was the last thing she felt.

"By the time you get back we'll have analysed the footage. And then we'll strike hard. This is just the start, you know that, right? Revelation will win this fight. We have to. Science has gone too far – you've seen it with your own eyes."

"I know." Her voice was flat and drained.

"Tess, come on. It's nearly over. Then you can have some time off, get your head straight, OK?"

No reply. It felt like nothing would ever be OK again.

"Look, I've got a surprise for you when you get back. I've pulled a few strings, got you a river-view suite. You've earned it."

Tess couldn't believe Blackwood could be so crass. Didn't he understand what she'd just witnessed?

"It's going to be difficult to keep Cillian quiet," she said, deliberately trying to puncture his mood.

"What do you mean?"

"He wants to go to the media."

"No."

"His mind's made up—"

"Then you have to *unmake* it. You know the plan. Stick to it."

"Maybe there's a different way—"

"What we're doing is the *only* way." Blackwood's voice allowed no room for doubt. "Tess, it's your job to make sure Cillian stays silent."

"But he's *not* on their side. He needs our help."

"What did you say?"

Tess could hear the alarm in Blackwood's voice. He couldn't bear the thought of her feeling any pity. "We need to help him," she said defiantly.

"That's the very last thing we should do—"

"I *want* to help him! The way he's been created, it's not his fault."

"On the surface they look so normal, but his confusion,

his vulnerability, it's to put you off guard. He's not like you and me."

"He's as angry as we are—"

"Tess, if you get drawn in, I won't be able to protect you."

"It's not like that—"

"If *you* fail, *I* fail. Is that what you want? I've gone out on a limb for you, defended you when others doubted—"

"How can you say that? After the things I've done?"

"If we lose this battle, it's not just Revelation that's finished, it's humanity. You mustn't lose your nerve, Tess."

"No-one could be more loyal than me!"

"But you have to prove it again. And again. Every day is a test for us. *Every* day. That's what it means to fight for a cause."

Tess could feel her mind clogging up with Blackwood's arguments.

"Foundation City is a fool's paradise," he urged. "It shows no respect for what's sacred. That's why we keep The Faith. Doubt is Weakness. Weakness is Failure. You're too good for that, Tess. Believe me."

# 47

Paige found Gabrielle roaming among the beautiful hard-wood hives of the apiary on P8's roof garden. In summer the air up there was so thick with bees it was impossible to get close to them, but once the temperatures dropped, the roof became one of Gabrielle's favourite places to come and think.

"You hear that?" she said as Paige approached. "That humming?"

Paige leant over one of the hives and heard a low, soothing drone coming from deep inside.

"That's the bees shivering, fluttering their wings to keep the queen warm. They do it all winter. That's their only job, to protect the queen."

"I think I'd have made a lousy bee," Paige said with a rueful smile.

"Oh..." Gabrielle sensed what was coming. "That doesn't sound good."

"I'm not sure this is for me any more ... what

we're doing in P8."

"After everything we've achieved? All the break-throughs?"

"When we started it was about medicine. About getting round stupid regulations that held back progress."

"Don't forget the millions of lives we saved through the Derespino vaccine," Gabrielle added. "Aren't you proud of that?"

"I suppose ... yes," Paige said. "But now..."

Gabrielle watched a couple of lone bees leave one of the hives for a few moments, then quickly dart back into the warmth. "You've been intimidated by Revelation's terror campaign."

"No."

"And that's exactly what they want. For people to live in fear of progress."

"I'm not frightened. But we shouldn't be doing this in secret any more," Paige said. "I thought by now everything would be above board."

"It's not that simple."

"The decisions we take in here –" Paige looked down into the cavernous light-filled atrium – "they're too big for us."

"You know what Einstein said about these?" Gabrielle rested her hand on one of the hives. "If the bee disappeared, then Man would have only 4 years of life left. No more bees, no more pollination, no more plants, no more animals, no more Man. It's apocryphal. It wasn't Einstein who said it at all. But people like to think it was because that way it's easier to believe. Otherwise it's just a crackpot theory. And it's the same with P8 – we're just like the bees. If we're shut down, human beings are finished long term."

"That's a big claim, Gabrielle."

"Believe me, the things we're creating here can save humanity from extinction for ever. But it could all be destroyed by ignorance."

"We're playing God with people's lives. That's not science."

"It's the highest form: it's creation. If we *can* use science to transform our existence, then we *must* use it. It's a moral imperative. The trouble is, people are terrified of creativity. To take a blank space and fill it with something new ... it's like magic, and it scares people because they can't control it. We're not composing symphonies or painting sunsets, we're creating with the building blocks of life."

"But if a painting fails, you can just burn it and start again."

"I know it's not easy. Sometimes there is a bit of ... ethical drift. But it's a price worth paying. You can't doubt that."

"So how much further will the ethics drift?"

"I wish I knew."

"Then at least tell me how much longer before we can come out of the shadows?"

"You have to make a choice, Paige. Do you want to be a creator and wield the power that goes with it? Do you want to be in the heat of this battle, with all its mess and chaos? Or do you want to stand on the sidelines and criticize?"

# 48

"I know how confusing it feels," Tess said quietly. "But we need to be smart about what we do next."

Cillian had been gazing out of the window, deep in his own thoughts ever since the Bullet Train had left the Northern Hub.

"Making wild accusations online isn't going to get us anywhere."

Cillian pulled his eyes away from the speeding blur of landscape and looked at Tess. "So we're just going to walk away? Pretend we didn't see anything?"

"No. Of course not."

"Then what?"

"These are dangerous people we're dealing with. Powerful organizations. We need to be careful."

"Foundation's a democracy. There are laws—"

"You think P8 cares about laws? It operates above them."

"That's bullshit. There is no 'above' the law."

"You think like that, you're putting your life in danger. And mine too."

It made Cillian hesitate. Tess was inextricably bound up in this now. Whatever he did next, she would be hit by the fallout.

"If we'd been caught in Gilgamesh," Tess said darkly, "we would've disappeared."

"All the more reason to blow this open."

"What if those experiments are linked to the military? They could have us arrested under anti-terror laws and we'd vanish. Just like those victims in their glass cells have vanished. Off the grid."

Cillian thought about the thousands of patients who poured into Gilgamesh Hospital every week without realizing what was going on a few metres away behind locked doors.

"And in any case, how free do you think our media really is?" Tess asked searchingly. "I saw it with my own eyes – our village wiped out by a virus, but the story everyone is told, the one everyone *believes* has only a grain of truth. The Derespino survivors didn't have a voice, no-one wanted to hear us. You have to understand, Cillian, the people we're up against, the ones your father worked for, they control the agenda. At best, you and I will end up as conspiracy nuts ranting on the Net."

"People's voices get heard in the end. That's how things change."

"In the end," Tess said. "But do we have that long? After what happened in Gilgamesh, we're marked men. Which is why we need to keep digging. Urgently. We need to name names. There's a whole web of scientists and money-men allowing this to happen, but they're only dangerous as long as they're anonymous. To fight your enemy you need to know who he is and how far he can reach."

"Which means we don't stand a chance on our own," Cillian insisted. "This is too big. Don't you get that?"

"The thing is..." Tess hesitated. "You were right. What you said in the Roadhouse. I'm not alone."

Cillian looked at her warily.

"There are people working with me. They know how to change things. How to take action."

"*People*? What people?"

"You have to trust me—"

"No, I don't. What people, Tess?"

"*I'm* the one who got us into Gilgamesh," she protested. "Isn't that proof enough?"

"Proof of what?" Cillian studied her face, trying to glimpse behind her easy expression. "Proof that you can get illegal weapons and hack databases. Who are you really?"

"After all we've been through? Seriously?"

"I barely know you." Cillian stared at her intently. "Everything you've told me could be lies."

"I work for people who won't stand by and watch," Tess replied, weighing each word carefully. "People who aren't dazzled by the wealth of Foundation City, who understand there's blood on the money, and that morality has been forgotten. People who have Faith."

Cillian felt his breathing momentarily stop. "Revelation..." he whispered.

"No."

"You're talking about Revelation—"

"Not everyone who gives their life to The Faith is a terrorist," Tess said quickly.

"Then who? *Who* are you talking about?"

173

"Cillian, they sent me to help you." She reached across the table to touch his hand, but he pulled away.

"We can put an end to what's going on, I swear. My people won't turn a blind eye to atrocities like the ones in Gilgamesh."

"And what about the atrocity of the Metro bomb?" he said angrily. "My father was murdered by those terrorists! How can you pretend to be better than them?"

"You don't understand—"

"You need to stay away from me." He stood up and stared at Tess, as if seeing her for the first time.

"Please listen—"

"Not to religious fanatics. Not that. Just stay away." Cillian turned and walked down the train corridor without even glancing back.

# 49

Hundreds of virtual tentacles reached out to embrace the Bullet Train as it crossed the City boundaries.

Tess glanced at her smartCell and saw the apps ping back to life: rolling news feeds and endlessly updated *What's Trending* lists, must-see must-hear must-read just a finger-touch away. But underneath all the froth, she knew that her smartCell was also reconnecting to Revelation's systems.

How would she explain her failure to Blackwood? He had trusted her, but she had blown it with Cillian, and Revelation took a very dim view of "non-fulfilment".

A few hours earlier she'd tried to patch things up. She'd gone to the restaurant car where Cillian was bunkered down in one of the booths, but he'd resolutely ignored her, and the last thing she wanted was to make a scene.

Now time was running out.

She gazed out of the window, trying to marshal her thoughts. The train snaked along viaducts through canyons of commercial banks and trading rooms, on its way to the terminal at Central West. It had been a bitterly cold night, coating the City with a thick layer of frost, and teams of bots were already hard at work blasting hot air onto the sidewalks.

The platform was her last chance to try and change Cillian's mind. Knowing she'd have to move fast, Tess got up and stood right by the carriage doors.

The train sighed to a stop and the *Door Unlocking* panel illuminated, but nothing happened.

Come on, open.

*"Thank you for travelling on the Bullet Train,"* the Virtual Conductor purred. *"If you are connecting to other transport networks, our advice-pods are located on the main concourse."*

OK, OK. Just open.

*"If you are terminating here, a wide range of dining and leisure facilities can be found on the first floor."*

Got it. Now open!

*"Whatever your plans, we wish you a very pleasant day."*

Finally the doors slid aside. Tess jumped down onto the platform and looked back along the train, searching for Cillian, but within seconds hundreds of people were flooding out of the carriages.

Tess waited in the middle of the platform, eyes scanning the crowds as they surged past.

There – over by the kiosks.

"Cillian! Wait!"

She tried to push through the crowds. "Don't go like this!"

But he wasn't stopping for anyone. Head down, refusing to listen or look at her, he vanished into the throng of commuters.

Tess's smartCell chirruped. It was Blackwood. He knew the Bullet Train had arrived: *What's your ETA @ Cotton Wharf?*

Not yet. She couldn't face Blackwood just yet. First she had to get her head straight.

As she made her way towards the network of escalators that criss-crossed the station, Tess had the unnerving feeling that everything had speeded up. Even though she'd only been away for a couple of days, the rawness of the landscape in the Provinces seemed to have reset her body-clock, and the frantic rush of City life now felt intimidating.

Aimlessly she rode the escalators up and down, trying to focus. She was terrified of how Revelation would react to her failure.

Worse, she was terrified of Cillian's revulsion. The Faith justified nothing in his eyes. He'd recoiled from her as if *she* was the monster.

# 50

Search again.

Search relentlessly.

Find evidence that was unassailable.

That was Cillian's only option now. People let you down and changed their stories, but hard evidence could always be trusted. Just like numbers.

It was difficult returning to the Residential Spire now, knowing what he did about his father. The building he'd always thought of as home suddenly seemed far less welcoming. Tentatively he swung open the apartment door...

A small police camera with blinking LEDs was perched on the bookshelf. 28-day monitoring after burglary was routine in case the intruders came back to finish off the job. But even though the camera was there for his own protection, Cillian felt as if he was being spied on.

He walked across the room, reached up and grabbed the camera. "How do you switch the thing off?" he muttered, hunting for the controls, before finally opening a drawer and tossing it inside. Quickly he checked the rest of the apartment, scooping up cameras in the kitchen and hallway, then he sat down at his father's workstation.

Go through everything again. That was the plan. It wasn't going to be easy. The patterns of evidence would be buried very deep.

Cillian clicked on *Main Documents*. Thousands of sub-folders scrolled across the screen, each containing dozens of files. Wrong way – that would take for ever.

He closed the window and did a search for encrypted sectors on the memory drives, then filtered the results, looking for shredded files.

*853 documents destroyed*. That was more like it. That was a number he could work with.

Cillian downloaded a Lazarus app, then set it running to reconstruct the digitally shredded data.

*Estimated time remaining: 47 minutes.*

Just long enough to get some toast and Marmite, and freshen up.

Standing in the shower, water tumbling down his face, Cillian's mind kept circling around Tess and his father, picking over memories, trying to understand how he had been so blind to what was really happening. Was it going to be like this for the rest of his life? Every time he trusted someone, was he going to end up getting hurt? When it came down to it, everyone seemed to be fighting their own battle.

As he turned the shower to power-pulse, Cillian noticed a thin, dark line on one of the tiles. Thinking it was a hair, he splashed some water over it, but it didn't budge. He looked closer, running his finger over the tile ... and realized it was a very thin fracture.

Cillian tapped it to see if water had got behind and loosened the plaster, when suddenly he noticed a similar crack on the tile below it ... and the next one. There was a line of cracks running from the shower head to the drain.

Had the City had an earth tremor while he was away?

He turned the shower off, pulled on a robe and stepped out of the cubicle. Cillian's eyes wandered suspiciously around the bathroom, then he relaxed his gaze and let his mind freewheel across the space...

The image snapped into focus—

*I see it.*

Tiles with hairline fractures were dotted around the bathroom, but *not randomly*. They were arranged on a grid: a neat grid that criss-crossed the walls and floor, linking the basin, the toilet, the shower and the drains.

Cillian approached the sink and peered into the gloom of the drain, but could only see water reflecting back. He grabbed a toothbrush, poked the plastic handle down and started sliding it around, feeling for irregularities.

Suddenly it caught on something.

Gently he eased the toothbrush up and saw a loom of very thin electrical cables. As he pulled, a whole length of wires emerged from the drain like a grotesque, high-tech worm. On the ends were 6 glass probes, each pulsing with a different colour.

Bewildered, Cillian grabbed his smartCell, photographed the probes and searched the Net for a match.

*BioMonitors.*

Probes to sample proteins and DNA from skin cells, sweat, mucus, blood and all the other things that get flushed and scrubbed from the human body.

He climbed back into the shower, lifted the grating and stuck his fingers down the drain: more probes.

Cillian turned the water supply off, flushed the toilet to empty it, then stuck his arm into the bowl as far as it would go, fingers groping around the porcelain bend ... until he felt another cluster of tiny glass probes embedded in the pipe.

Pulling on his jeans, he scrambled to the kitchen and returned with a toolkit. He grabbed the hammer and swung it against the toilet, punching jagged holes in the china bowl until it shattered ... to reveal a sinister loom of wires emerging from the drainpipe.

Possessed with a compulsion to reveal the entire pattern, Cillian started swinging wildly at the walls, smashing tiles, hacking out grooves to uncover a network of wires buried in the brickwork, converging on a single point in the subfloor. Cillian ripped the last tile away, levered up a metal cavity plate ...

And found a ControlBox flickering with lights, sending data down the line to an unseen server.

*It was still live.*

Proof. This was exactly the proof he needed. Covert surveillance. Violation of civil liberties. They'd have to take him seriously now.

He grabbed his smartCell—

And hesitated.

Who could he call?

Detective Qin? The man who had regarded him with such suspicion after the burglary?

His father's lawyer, who had an air about him that he knew far more than he was saying?

Hailey? The ice queen from the Walk-In?

None of them could be trusted, and Cillian knew if he made the wrong move now, he might find himself waking up in a glass cell in Gilgamesh, vanished for ever. If he was going to sacrifice himself to expose the truth, he needed to be sure that his voice would be heard.

He looked at the ControlBox blinking calmly in the floor cavity. Where was it sending the data?

Gilgamesh?

Somewhere else?

Who could put a trace on it?

Who did he know for sure was *not* part of the P8 conspiracy?

# 51

Tess watched anxiously as the electronic indicator counted down the stops to Cotton Wharf. There were only so many times she could ignore Blackwood's messages. Sooner or later she would have to face the consequences of her failure.

As the tram slowed, she steeled herself and prepared to get off, when suddenly her smartCell pinged again.

This time it wasn't Blackwood. It was Cillian.

*Is it true about my enemy's enemy?*

Maybe there was still a way through this.

*Yes,* she tapped back quickly. *Definitely.*

*Then you need to see this.*

Tess slumped down in the seat, light-headed with relief. A second chance.

"The tools," Cillian said. "That's why the intruder had tools. I think he was going to retrieve these probes."

Tess stared at the smashed-up bathroom and looms

of cable, stunned by the depth of the surveillance.

"No wonder my father never wanted to move apartments. It would have ruined his experiment. Whatever I was doing – showering, having a piss, cleaning my teeth – everything was being analysed. Seems I've never had a private life."

"Well now it's going to help us." Tess slid a touch-pad from her rucksack, powered it up and knelt down by the ControlBox. "This will take us right into the heart of P8's systems. Finally we can see who they really are."

Cillian frowned as she jumped a lead into one of the inputs and started to upload tracing software. "I doubt that'll work. It'll all be encrypted."

"The data will be, but not the path it takes. This inserts a marker into the digital-stream. It's like injecting dye. If we let it run for long enough, it'll give us a map of the entire network. Right back to the source." She tapped the screen to activate the program, and lines of code scrolled into view.

For a few moments they stared at the display, then Tess turned to Cillian. "You did the right thing, telling me."

"Did I?"

"Until we find out how far this reaches, we can't trust the authorities. Any of them."

"And we can trust 'your people'? Terrorists?" Cillian studied her intently.

"What happened to your father ... the Metro bomb, that was a tragedy," Tess said quietly. "It should never have happened. But there's a bigger battle being fought here. Science is destroying innocent lives. You and I have seen it, and we need to focus on that."

Cillian's mind flashed back to the strange, mutated children in their glass cells. "My father really was in way too deep," he said quietly.

"Maybe." Tess could see the pain on his face as he finally started to accept the truth.

They gazed at the screen in silence, watching the data unfurl.

But gradually, as the markers pinged back locations, Tess realized it wasn't just the pathways to the control servers that were being mapped, it was every other node on the system as well.

*Every experimental subject.*

And Cillian saw it too. "Shit ... I'm not the only one out here, am I?"

"I don't know," Tess said.

But she did.

She knew that this list tore open the heart of P8. As the data settled, she quickly unplugged the touch-pad. "I need to get it analysed."

"I'm coming with you."

"No."

"Why?"

"The safest thing is for you to stay visible."

Cillian could hear the alarm in her voice. "What do you mean?"

"Leave the apartment, but don't go back to the university. Keep away from anywhere they'd expect you to be. Stay in busy places, somewhere public with lots of people. I'll contact you when I've got some answers."

"But—"

"Do it! Just do what I say. Please." Tess grabbed the tablet and hurried from the apartment.

# 52

"I was right," Blackwood whispered, unable to tear his eyes away from the data-map growing across the Wall-Screen. "They're really out there. All their living experiments, walking the streets of the City."

The passion in his voice filled Tess with dread. "What about P8?" she asked, trying to keep Blackwood on track. "The markers still can't get through their firewalls."

"Right now, I don't care." He turned to Tess and cradled her face gently in his hands. "You've given me Generation Zero. All of them. Every last one."

"I thought the whole point was to get inside P8."

Blackwood pointed to a sub-menu where the program was compiling a list of identifiers in alphanumeric code. "Each one of these is a person who has no idea what they really are. Who thinks they just don't quite fit in, or have some strange obsession. Now we can root out this evil." His eyes were bright with anticipation. "You've given us the Kill List. Mutations like this can't be allowed to exist.

Who knows what they might be capable of doing?"

Tess said nothing; she turned to the WallScreen and gazed at the numbers, wondering which one was Cillian.

"You should be happy."

"I am." But her eyes weren't smiling.

"There can be no exceptions, Tess. We must destroy them all before they infiltrate, breed and corrupt the wider population."

"He's still useful—"

"He's served his purpose. We've got more from Cillian than we could have imagined—"

"But there's much more he could do for us—"

"And now you have to kill him."

His words punched the breath out of Tess. The heavy silence between them lingered as she desperately tried to think of a way to change Blackwood's mind.

"He's innocent," she said finally.

"None of them are innocent."

"He hasn't *done* anything."

"It's not what he's done. It's what he *is*. They've been created for vanity and profit, and they will destroy everything it means to be human. Which is why they must be *uncreated*."

"There must be another way," Tess pleaded. "What about the media? Now we've got proof, we can expose everything—"

"It won't work." Blackwood was adamant. "Everyone wants to be smarter, stronger, more immune, more beautiful. If we expose P8, we'll just be telling the whole world what they've achieved, and any chance of stopping them will be lost."

"Decent people won't tolerate their cruelty."

"You really think 'decent people' care when it comes

187

to their child's cancer? Or not ageing for another 30 years? Or being able to out-think their rivals? Foundation is a city of the wealthy. They'll be queuing up to buy genetic cures and enhancements. Once people take control of their own genome and bend it to their will, society will split from top to bottom. The rich will take everything; they'll get stronger and healthier. The poor will be left with nothing but disease and death. How can that be right?"

"How can murdering Cillian be right?"

"It's not murder to kill what should never have been born. Remember, the Creator made all humans equal." Blackwood pointed to the Kill List. "Destroying these is the only way to honour that."

"I don't want Cillian to die. Please. That's all I know."

"*You* don't want—" There was disbelief in Blackwood's voice. "*You*. All these years I've nurtured you, and you'd turn against me?"

"It's not like that—"

"I saved you, Tess. I plucked you from a life of hopeless rejection. And this is how you repay me? By betraying me … for a monster?"

Tess looked into his unyielding eyes and finally started to understand.

"You knew, didn't you?" she whispered. "You knew what the bomb was going to do. But you wanted bloodshed and carnage—"

"How can you even think that?"

"You *wanted* it!"

"All I've ever asked is that you do the right thing. And I'm telling you now, unless we act, the Fall of Man will happen in *our* lifetimes. But if you're not strong enough –" he looked at her with a dark sense of disappointment – "then there's no place for you here."

Tess was stunned. "You'd really turn your back on me?"

"It's the other way around. But be careful what you decide. I don't know how long you think you could last out there without Revelation to protect you. Without me."

There was nothing Tess could say, no argument left that could save both her and Cillian.

One of them was finished.

# 53

The stone floor was cold and hard on her knees, but Tess didn't care. She deserved to feel pain.

Just a week ago she'd been in this very church on a mission to single out Cillian. Then the lines of right and wrong had been so clearly drawn, then he had just been a target, but now ... now he was real.

Vividly real.

All her life, Tess had felt the presence of a greater power watching over her, protecting her. Why else had she been spared from the Derespino Virus when so many had died? Who but the Creator could have saved her? That was what had drawn her to Revelation's powerful interpretation of The Faith: at its centre was a God of action and justice who didn't flinch from conflict and struggle.

A radical God.

But now Tess had glimpsed a terrible flaw: for Revelation, The Faith was a religion of judgement, which meant it would always be a religion of blood.

She looked up at the icon that loomed over the altar. Despite the violence and horror of the death it depicted, hadn't people once seen this icon as a symbol of love and forgiveness? Of tolerance not vengeance?

Maybe it was precisely because it was quieter and gentler that this understanding of The Faith had become so hollowed out and marginalized, usurped by the fervour of Revelation.

But what was the true interpretation?

Tess clasped her hands together and reached out, praying to the Creator as a god of love, not vengeance, begging for His help in unravelling the deadly knot that had trapped her.

In the silence of the cavernous church she listened for salvation ... but all she heard were her own doubts echoing back.

Tess slumped down.

Deep in her heart she knew it was too late. After everything she had done, all the blood that was on her hands, she was beyond redemption. Even a god of love could not overlook her sins.

Tess's smartCell beeped. The message was stark and simple: *Eugene Rosner.*

It meant the gun was ready.

Following Revelation was the only thing left for her; all other doors were closed. Tess had lived by their version of The Faith; she would have to die by it.

And kill by it.

# 54

A hit inside the City demanded special precautions.

A printed gun could be burnt, rendering it untraceable, but that risked making the police focus even more attention on the body, which was the last thing Tess wanted. Far better to confuse the investigation from the outset.

Because of its wealth, Foundation City was constantly targeted by organized gangs from the Continent, who got rich supplying young traders with anything and everything they desired. One of the main thrusts of criminal policing was to keep these gangs out of Foundation, and a huge amount of time and money was spent tracking foreign weapons and operators. Using a known gun from the Continent, combined with the strange burglary at Cillian's apartment the previous week, should put the investigation nicely on the wrong track.

Forcing herself not to think about anything but practical details, Tess pushed open the rusty gate of the walled cemetery that sat in the shadow of a football stadium. It had been spared by developers only to be forgotten by the faithful, and few people came here any more. Even so, it wouldn't be suspicious to see someone wandering among the graves, which made it the perfect dead drop.

Slowly Tess walked up and down the crooked rows, trudging through pristine snow, checking the names on each tomb, until she came to a small granite cube with a faded brass plate: Eugene Rosner.

Tess knelt down, brushed the powdery snow aside, placed a pebble on the tomb as a mark of respect, then gently pressed the nameplate. It clicked open, revealing a small chamber.

Inside was the gun, a modified Luger.

She picked it up and turned on the power. The pistol grip pulsed red for a few seconds while it identified her DNA, pre-programmed into the weapon by the armourers at Revelation.

There was a gentle *ping*, then the handle glowed blue.

Ready for the kill.

# 55

Cillian climbed the final steps and emerged onto an exterior viewing platform perched on top of the Baroque dome of the Cathedral of Veneration.

Snow was falling heavily, but with no wind it felt eerily gentle. He crossed the walkway, sat on a bench at the Skyline Bakery Bar under one of the heaters and ordered a latte and a warm muffin.

Looking around, he immediately understood why Tess had chosen to meet here. The platform was bustling with school kids who crowded around Hologram Stations, exploring how the City skyline had changed across the centuries. Crowds meant safety, and right now Cillian knew it was impossible to be too paranoid.

Like many other church buildings, the cathedral had long since stopped being anything to do with religion, and developers had turned it into a state-of-the-art gallery-museum complex.

Foundation City placed huge emphasis on culture

and learning, and generous tax breaks meant that banks were always eager to invest in these showpieces. For years this had been one of Cillian's favourites, but coming back now, everything felt different. The whole building seemed to be just one big lie. He wondered how the financiers who were so keen to put their names to places like this *really* made their money. Foundations were always built on somebody's bones.

Cillian hoped that the scandal he and Tess were about to reveal would turn Foundation City inside out; but he was afraid. Tempted by wonder-drugs and the miracles promised by radical genetic editing, would anyone be willing to make a stand? And once people knew what he really was, would they reject him? Or worse, hunt him down?

It was impossible to think through the repercussions; there were too many unknowns. He would just have to face what was coming with grim determination. At least now he wasn't alone.

Cillian checked his smartCell. She was late.

Picking up his coffee, he walked over to the viewing rail and peered down through the falling snow. Thousands of people hurried across Cathedral Plaza. He'd never see Tess coming.

# 56

For once the Clearing-Bots couldn't keep up with the heavy snowfall. It made walking quickly impossible, which just prolonged Tess's ordeal.

She plugged earphones into her smartCell and flooded her head with music, trying to drive out all doubts.

*There is Only One Faith.*

*Right is On My Side.*

*Doubt is Weakness.*

She repeated the phrases over and over like a mantra, refusing to give any headspace to the Cillian who had trusted her.

*There is Only One Faith.*

*Right is On My Side.*

*Doubt is Weakness.*

As she crossed Cathedral Plaza she looked up at the once-magnificent old building now festooned with ultra-modern steel and glass additions. The developers had done all they could to remove The Faith from this building.

But they hadn't quite succeeded...

Tess reached into her pocket and ran her fingers over an old key; there were still some hidden parts of the Cathedral of Veneration that could be redeemed.

Cillian was already waiting for her, paper coffee cup in hand.

"Tess!" he hurried over.

"Hey." She focussed hard on trying to be casual.

"Coffee?"

She shook her head. "I'm fine."

Cillian lowered his voice. "So how did it go? What did they find?"

Tess glanced anxiously at the other people on the viewing platform. "It's easier if I show you."

"What's wrong?"

"Nothing. It's just..."

He looked at her with such anticipation and trust.

"You'll see. Come on."

The wooden steps leading down from the viewing platform threaded between the inner and outer skins of the huge dome, winding around dozens of stone pillars. It was like walking through the building's skeleton.

Just beyond the halfway point, Tess ducked under the handrail and followed a narrow ledge around the curve of the dome. Cillian followed her as they headed into the gloom, disappearing from the public areas.

Abruptly she stopped, took the key from her pocket, unlocked a small wooden door and pushed it open to reveal a spiral stone staircase.

"Seriously?" Cillian peered down into the shaft that was illuminated by occasional narrow slits.

"It's how the bell ringers used to get up and down without being seen."

"Where exactly are we going, Tess?"

"Somewhere safe."

And she led the way...

Down and down...

Inside the massive stone walls...

Past the crypt with its boutiques and sushi bars...

Down into the darkness of the cathedral's ancient foundations.

# 57

Tess opened the door onto a deep, menacing hum.

Stretched out before them was a power chamber built into the catacombs; all the electricity collected from panels on the dome was stored here in hundreds of massive batteries, then recycled back into the Cathedral's grid.

"Tess, what's going on?"

"You'll see." She stepped out onto one of the walkways running between the lines of grey power cells.

Her evasiveness made Cillian feel uneasy, but he knew he had to see this through. There was no going back to his old life, and no-one got answers by running away.

So he stepped onto the gantry and followed her.

The air was oppressive with the tension of stored electricity. It was like being on the verge of a conflagration, as if the slightest disturbance would trigger catastrophe.

Cillian watched the muscles in her back moving, listened to the click of her footsteps on the metal treads.

He knew the cadence of her body so well, how she walked, how her head moved as she observed the room. Yet something about Tess now seemed unreachable, as if she had thrown up an invisible barrier between them.

"If your people don't want to get involved, we'll find another way," he said, trying to get a reaction.

"I don't think that would be so smart."

Just for a moment he heard regret in her voice.

"In another world, Cillian, I think we could have had something. But we're not in another world." Tess stopped walking. "And in this one ..." She turned, arm outstretched, Luger pointing straight at his head. "I have to kill you."

React.

He had to react—

To defend himself—

But Cillian was paralysed.

With shock.

With fear.

With sadness.

"Revelation..." he breathed the word softly, finally understanding that *he* had been the enemy all along.

"You should never have trusted me," Tess said, blinking back tears that pricked her eyes. "I begged them to find another way. But they wouldn't." She tightened her grip on the gun. "You don't belong here. I'm sorry ... you should never have existed."

Suddenly Cillian's world slipped. Time beat to an intensely slow rhythm; he saw the veins pulse in Tess's wrist like the tick of a grandfather clock; he felt the electricity swirling around their bodies like water; he saw her eyes blink once, slow and serene. In this dimension he could reach up and take the gun before she fired. He could get out of this alive.

But what was the point?

He had trusted his father, and had been lied to his whole life. He had trusted Tess, and it was about to earn him a bullet in the head. Suddenly Cillian was flooded with a deep weariness. How many more layers of deception were there? If betrayal was all life had to offer, what was the point of fighting to survive?

Maybe he really didn't belong in this world.

Maybe she was right.

And maybe this was the way it should end.

As Cillian made his decision, time caught up again.

"It's all right, Tess."

She tensed her finger, steeling herself for the kill. "Fight," she hissed.

"No."

"Fight!"

"Just do what you have to." Cillian drew a final breath.

*There is Only One Faith.*

Tess willed herself to squeeze the trigger.

*Doubt is Weakness.*

To finish the job.

*Right is On My side.*

But it didn't feel like right. It felt like cold-blooded murder.

It felt like hate.

"What a disappointment." The voice cut across the silence.

Tess spun round and saw Blackwood emerge from the darkness between the power cells.

"There are so many weak people in the world, Tess. But I never thought you were one of them."

"Don't do this," she said. "It's wrong."

Blackwood raised his arm so that the laser sights of

his Glock 52 projected a red dot onto Cillian's forehead. "That's the trouble with thinking too much: it makes you hesitate." His finger tensed on the trigger. "And hesitation is always a mistake."

"Please – let him live!"

"Watch and learn."

"NO!"

*CRACK! CRACK!*

The shots echoed around the power chamber.

Cillian waited for the pain to sear through his head, for hot sticky blood to explode across his face—

But it didn't.

A gasp spat from Blackwood's mouth, his eyes glazed with disbelief and he dropped heavily to his knees, revealing a spray of red on the wall behind him.

For a baffling moment Cillian couldn't work out what was happening. He looked at Tess, still gripping the gun, holding her aim on Blackwood ... who crumpled forwards onto the metal walkway. The back of his head had been blown away.

Tess swayed with nausea. She stared at Blackwood's twitching body, barely able to believe what she'd done.

Cillian reached out to steady her, but she backed away like a frightened animal.

"Run!" she screamed.

"No!"

"I can't help you any more!"

"Then let me help *you*!"

"Get out of the City!" Tess swung around so that the gun was pointing at Cillian's head. "Before I kill you as well."

Her voice was cold and hard, and Cillian knew she would do it, but still he didn't run. "I won't leave you."

Tess squeezed the trigger—

But her finger never completed its move.

With impossible speed Cillian's hand lashed out and knocked the gun aside.

Tess felt her knees buckle, but Cillian caught her.

A howl burst from her lungs. "Leave me!"

"No."

"I don't deserve to live."

"*He* didn't deserve to live." Cillian looked at Blackwood's bloodied corpse. "*He* didn't."

"I followed him," Tess whispered in shame.

"Not in the end." Cillian lifted her up and slammed her against one of the power cells, trying to shock her to her senses. "Now you need to focus!"

# 58

"How do we get out of this?" Cillian demanded.

Tess just stared at Blackwood's body splayed on the metal walkway, limbs twisted, blood oozing from his head.

"*What was your plan?*" Cillian shook her. "How were you going to get away?"

Before she could stop herself, Tess vomited.

"It's OK." He put his arm around her, holding her until she stopped retching. "You can do this. But you have to focus."

She nodded.

Training.

This is what she'd been trained for, to deal with chaos and havoc.

She pushed Cillian aside and stood on her own two feet, breathing deeply, getting her balance again.

Training.

Turn off emotions and focus on the cold, hard facts. The victim had changed, but the plan could still hold.

"Dissociate from the body," she said, forcing herself back on track.

Cillian looked at her blankly. "Meaning?"

"Meaning we were never here." She held up the Luger and clicked *Erase Personal Profile* on the grip's menu, then watched the LEDs blink as the gun started to reformat.

"You're leaving it here?" He still wasn't convinced she was thinking straight.

"Just shut up and do as I say." Tess handed him a small canister. "Spray this on everything we've touched. Especially on the puke."

"What is it?"

"DNA compound. Turns biological traces into a meaningless soup. It'll confuse forensics."

Hurriedly Cillian retraced their steps, spraying everything they'd touched.

"Keep some for the gun," Tess called out.

He ran back. The Luger had finished reformatting and Tess dropped it onto the metal treads. Cillian discharged the spray over it until there was nothing left. "Enough?"

"It'll have to be." Tess slid the Luger into a pool of Blackwood's blood, swirled it around with her toe, then kicked it off the gantry so that it clattered onto the concrete floor below. "When the police find it, they'll just think it was lost in the struggle."

Cillian didn't know if she was being smart or stupid; he was way out of his depth. "What next?"

"Get out."

"Same way we came?"

Tess shook her head. "Too much CCTV."

"Shit. CCTV..." Cillian looked up and saw cameras dotted across the power chamber ceiling. "They've seen everything."

"We disabled these, parachuted a software bug into the system."

"How do you know it worked?"

"Because if it hadn't, we'd be under arrest by now." She grabbed Cillian and started running to the far side of the power chamber, where the gantry fed into a loading bay with winches and pulleys clustered around a series of steeply sloping chutes.

"It's how they replace dead power cells," Tess said, climbing into the bottom of Chute 3. "But they hardly ever get used."

They crawled up the metal shaft and came to a security grille at the top. The lock had already been cut, and it slid back easily ... to reveal a blinding snowstorm outside.

They were momentarily lost. Roads, lawns, paths were all vanishing under muffling snow. Stumbling over disappearing graves, they made it to some iron railings, hauled themselves over, and were finally absorbed by the crowds slipping across Cathedral Plaza.

Cillian glanced around, searching for any sign of flashing lights or alarms. "Where's the safest place?"

Suddenly the enormity of what lay ahead crashed in on Tess. "Nowhere's safe," she whispered.

"There must be somewhere—"

"We have to vanish. Disappear *completely*."

"But we've covered our tracks—"

"Cillian! We're not just running from the police. We're running from Revelation! They know what I look like, how I operate, who my friends are. They know *everything* about me. When I killed Blackwood, I signed my own death warrant. Neither of us is safe any more."

# 59

Urgently glancing over their shoulders to see if they were being followed, Cillian and Tess ran into the labyrinthine Kasbah Quarter. They turned left and right at random, losing themselves in winding alleys lined with trendy juice bars and psychic reading parlours.

"Give me your smartCell," Tess said. "We have to run silent."

He handed it over, and immediately she prised off the back, popped out the battery and dropped the cell down the nearest drain grating.

"Couldn't you just turn it off?"

"Not enough." She ripped out the motherboard, broke it in pieces and tossed the bits down the next grating. "All smartCells have passive RFID chips. They ping listening posts right across the City. The Net's tapping in 24/7."

Nimbly her fingers dismantled her own smartCell and scattered the pieces, until she just held the 2 micro-chips. "We have to obliterate these."

She clasped Cillian's hand and discreetly pressed the chips into his palm. "Wait for my signal." Then she led the way across the road and headed towards a roast chestnut stand.

"2 bags of honey-coated," Tess said, eyeing the glowing coals.

The seller scratched his dirty beard as he spooned some sweet goo onto a hotplate, then he glanced up with a familiar smile. "Don't worry, it won't be as bad as you think."

"What?" Tess hadn't expected conversation.

"That frown on your face. Whatever put it there won't turn out to be so bad. You'll see."

"I wouldn't be so sure."

"Trust me. I've had this stall 32 years. Seen 'em walk past, all frowning, the world on their shoulders, everything so urgent."

"32 years ... that's a lot of chestnuts."

"Too many to count." The seller nodded. "I tell you, life goes on whatever."

As he turned away to rummage for a couple of small paper bags, Tess squeezed Cillian's hand, and he dropped the microchips into the hot coals.

The seller spooned the chestnuts into the bags and handed them over. "Should do the trick."

"Thanks." Tess gave him some money, then turned and hurried away with Cillian.

As she led the way into one of the cloistered alleys, Tess reached into her pocket and pulled out a pair of sunglasses. "Where are yours?"

"But it's snowing."

"It's not a fashion statement. Put them on."

"I haven't got any with me."

"Then make sure you avoid eye contact with the bill-boards." Tess pointed to a tram shelter further along the street. "They do retinal scans as you pass."

"It's not the ad agencies we're running from."

"Who knows where the data is sent. Or who's hacked their servers." She glared at him. "I'm not joking."

Hurriedly Cillian wrapped his scarf around his face and looked down, focussing his gaze on the deep foot-prints in the snow.

They emerged from the Kasbah onto one of the main shopping boulevards that radiated from Olympic Piazza. Normally it would be thronged with people, but the storm had driven most of them indoors, abandoning the pavements to Cleaning-Bots struggling to clear snow.

"The one time you need crowds..." Cillian said edgily.

"Anyone tracking us will still be looking in the Kasbah. At least for now." Tess pointed down one of the glitzy boulevards. "Let's try that way."

Hugging the line of shopfronts, they made their way towards the Piazza. With every step, Tess's paranoia started to infect Cillian, until his senses were bristling. He studied the trickle of pedestrians walking in the opposite direction, scrutinizing each one for any tell-tale signs of malice, but now they all looked sinister.

"How will they come for us?" he asked.

"I wish I knew."

The guttural roar of a motorcycle engine revved to their left. Tess spun around and saw a biker cruis-ing down the centre of the road, snow churning in his wheels. His eyes locked onto them.

Tess gripped Cillian's hand and tried to walk faster, but the motorcycle kept pace.

"Inside," she whispered, and pulled Cillian towards

the palatial glass entrance of an upmarket department store.

It was like entering a parallel universe – a wall of warmth, shiny displays and beautiful shop assistants in immaculate clothes. For a few moments it seemed inconceivable that they were running for their lives. Cillian closed his eyes and breathed in the heady scents wafting around the cosmetics hall. It felt so safe and reassuring—

"Let's cut through to the service roads." Tess's voice jolted him back to reality.

They hurried past shoppers browsing jewellery and leather goods, then pushed through some little-used swing doors leading back outside.

The street was deserted, the snow lay deep and undisturbed. It would be a while until the bots got round to clearing these alleys.

Heads down, collars up, keeping as low a profile as possible, they started to hurry away, but had barely gone 10 paces when a 4x4 pulled up sharply across the end of the street.

The doors opened and 3 men got out. "It's all right, Cillian," one of them said. "You can trust us."

"Just step away from the girl," a man in a grey suit instructed. "Let us deal with her."

# 60

"Run!" Tess grabbed Cillian's arm and pulled him back down the alley.

"Cillian, you're making a mistake!" one of the men shouted. "We're here to protect you."

"They're lying!" Tess urged.

Cillian glanced over his shoulder, but strangely the men weren't chasing them. "Are they police?"

"No."

"Revelation?"

Tess shook her head. "We'd be dead by now."

They heard the powerful roar of an engine. Moments later an armoured security van swerved round the corner and sped towards them, cutting off their escape route. It skidded to a halt, the doors burst open and men in dark fatigues spilled out of the back, fanning across the road.

"Cillian, you need to trust us," the man in the suit called from the other end of the alley.

"No, you don't!" Tess span around, desperately

looking for another way out. But it was useless. Figures were closing in from all sides.

"*She's* the danger, not us," the suit warned. "We're on your side. Don't let her trick you again!"

"Don't listen to him."

"You're safe now," the suit said calmly. "We won't harm you."

Cillian turned and looked at him ... he seemed so normal—

Until he drew the gun.

"No!" Cillian yelled.

The bullet cracked through the alley and Tess slumped forward, her blood spattering across the snow.

"NO!"

Time slipped a gear.

Furious energy surged through Cillian's body.

He rushed for the man in the suit. He would take them out. All of them. It would be easy—

Until a searing pain erupted in the small of his back and he stumbled.

He reached back and felt a steel dart, deeply embedded into his skin.

Desperate to stop whatever chemical was flooding his bloodstream, he yanked it out, feeling his flesh tear.

THUNK! THUNK! 2 more darts were fired into his shoulders.

A surge of defiance welled up inside him.

He leapt across the alley, grabbed one of the men and hurled him through the air.

"Restraints!" a voice shouted.

Suddenly a cold steel collar clamped around Cillian's neck. He heard the hydraulics whine as the collar tightened, crushing his airway.

"And again!"

Another metallic *clang* and a collar clamped around his right leg. Cillian turned to see 3 men holding a pole attached to it, pulling his leg from under him.

Desperately he tried to fight them off, but the more he struggled, the tighter they closed in.

So this is what it came to: being hunted down like an animal.

He saw Tess's bleeding body being carried towards the security van. Somehow he had to help her, but the weakness inside was spreading so fast he couldn't even stand up.

The men dragged him through the snow, following the trail of Tess's blood.

He tried to dig his feet in, but they just slid hopelessly on the ice.

One final dart—

And everything went black.

# 61

The instant he woke, Cillian knew he'd been here before.

He was in a glass cube that was a disturbing mix of child's bedroom and laboratory.

Monitoring screens and cartoon characters jostled for wall space, the small bed was rigged with a host of biological sensors, the plastic toys scattered across the floor all had embedded LEDs that blinked as they sent data streams to a control plinth outside the cube.

It was as if childhood innocence had been smashed into cutting edge science.

Cillian peered into the gloom beyond the glass walls and could make out similar cubes dotted across a vast floor, but they were all empty.

Gilgamesh.

He must be back in Gilgamesh, a prisoner in one of those degenerate wards.

Hunting for clues, he looked up through the glass ceiling, the only link with the outside world, and stared at the moonlit clouds being driven silently past on freezing winds. A few seconds later he saw the reassuring flicker of aircraft lights passing overhead, coming in to land. This wasn't the barren sky of the Provinces; he was still in Foundation City.

Somewhere.

He sat on the edge of the small bed and studied the room: carved squirrels on the 4 corners of the bedstead ... a duvet cover, pale blue with pictures of old cars. His gaze darted across the toys perched on every surface. There were different shaped bricks that fitted together in a colourful puzzle, a plastic ball studded with push buttons, a wooden train track with bridges and tunnels, penny racers, a bright yellow excavator...

And as he looked, Cillian felt his fingers twitch. They *knew* what to do with each of these toys. That red sports car – if you pressed the roof, it made an engine sound and flashed its lights; the model robot – if you flipped it upside down and folded the limbs, it became a spaceship.

A clockwork mobile hung above the bed, sheep jumping over a fence. He reached out and pulled the string. "Old MacDonald" chimed soothingly.

And he knew that sound.

Not just the tune, but that *exact* sound, with the 2 flat notes...

It opened the floodgates.

Images cascaded from his subconscious—

*I see it.*

Rich patterns of memories suddenly illuminated, and Cillian knew what every inch of this floor looked like right down to the last scuff-mark.

He knew how the shadows fell throughout the day.

He remembered adults coming in and out, some to

play or talk or sing to him, others to give him injections or plug him up to machines with glowing displays.

Memory triggered memory, building intricate, detailed patterns, creating such an intense feeling of belonging that he knew for sure...

*This was once his room.*

This was where the missing years of his life had been spent; everything before his third birthday belonged in here.

It was as if a door that had been stubbornly closed all his life had been suddenly thrown open, and the torrent of memories temporarily washed away all other concerns.

Cillian felt joy, relief and an overwhelming sense of nostalgia as he reconnected.

He sank to his knees, buried his face in his hands and sobbed.

# 62

"We've kept it exactly as it was on the day you left."

Cillian looked up and saw a tall, elegant woman with blonde hair, standing in the cube.

"Cosy, isn't it?" She smiled with eyes that were somehow older than the rest of her face.

Cillian knew that smile: he'd seen it before, a long time ago.

"I'm sorry we had to intervene," Gabrielle said. "We'd much rather you were independent, making your own choices, that's the whole point of this stage. But your life was in danger and you're far too valuable to lose."

All the warmth of belonging drained away, as Cillian remembered being captured on the street and dragged into the security van. Instinctively he reached to the small of his back, feeling for the wound left by the dart. It wasn't there.

"They told me it got a bit rough," Gabrielle said, as if reading his mind. "But you've healed well."

"How long have I been here?"

"Just tonight."

"That doesn't make sense." His hand felt for the wound again, but there was no dressing. His flesh was smooth and complete.

"A little bit of biotech we're working on," Gabrielle said with a mischievous smile. "Pretty impressive, even if I say it myself."

Cillian looked at her warily.

"So what's it like to be home?" Her arm swept expansively across the high-tech cube.

"You didn't have to kidnap me."

"Having visitors isn't really P8's style," Gabrielle said casually. "We need to keep things secure."

P8. That was where he had ended up. Finally. Cillian felt sick as he remembered the ControlBox in his bathroom, greedily sucking in data year after year. "Aren't you ashamed of what you're doing?"

"I couldn't be more proud." Gabrielle studied his eyes intently. "Especially when I look at you."

Who was this stranger? Cillian's mind raced to remember her face, but it kept eluding him.

"It's been 13 years," Gabrielle said. "I looked a little different then."

It was unnerving how she seemed able to read his mind.

"I ran the team that raised you. Here. In this very room. But it wasn't just about the science. Some of my DNA was used to build you."

"What are you talking about?" Cillian edged away.

"Paul and I shared the same vision. It made sense to work together."

"*You're* my mother?"

"A rather outdated, simplistic concept." Gabrielle smiled. "The future will be about strains of DNA that are designed and perfected. But if you really want to be sentimental … I suppose you could see me like that."

Gabrielle stepped forwards and put her arms around him. Gently her hands touched his face … she breathed in his smell … for a few moments it felt like a maternal embrace—

Then with a jolt Cillian realized. She was scrutinizing him. Like a specimen.

He disentangled himself. "Where's Tess?"

"She's being looked after."

"I want to see her."

"All in good time. First you need to see *yourself*."

"What are you talking about?"

"There's no rush. We've got plenty of time—"

"No!"

His sharp note of defiance caught Gabrielle off guard. "You should rest awhile."

"Whatever you've got to tell me, tell me *now*."

Gabrielle ran her fingers through her hair. "No problems with your self-esteem," she muttered. "All right. I'll show you what you really are."

# 63

"No babies were ever as well loved as these," Gabrielle said with pride.

There were 10 glass cribs evenly spaced around the room, each one containing a tiny infant. Multiple cameras captured every second of their young lives, while sensors and probes fed streams of data back to arrays of computers and monitoring screens. But it was the RoboNurses looming over the incubators that transfixed Cillian.

Each one was a complex robotic arm that fussed over its charge with infinite patience, gently adjusting the sleeping position, delicately changing nappies, stroking the infant with cotton wool when it was distressed. There was even an option to hum soothing nursery rhymes.

"Was it like this for me?" Cillian tried to remember what it felt like to be nursed by a mechanical arm that rocked you to sleep with digital audio.

"Of course. From the moment of conception, as a

foetus, then as an infant in your cube, you were genetically accelerated."

"Normal just wasn't good enough?"

"Normal is disease and death. Normal is cancer and pain, disability and dementia," Gabrielle clarified. "That's what started all this – the dream of liberating us from disease. But the deeper we dug into the genome, the more remarkable we found it. If there ever was a God, he hid all his miracles inside the double helix of DNA."

Gabrielle smiled as she used a touchpad on the side of an incubator to tickle the baby inside. "Once we'd glimpsed what was possible, it would have been ignorant to stop. We had to keep going."

"The screening room's ready," Cole announced.

Cillian turned and saw a man scrutinizing him.

"This is Cole. One of my assistants," Gabrielle said. "There's not much he doesn't know about you already."

"Think of me as your guardian angel," Cole said with a wry smile.

"We've prepped a few home movies to fill in the gaps." Gabrielle ushered Cillian towards a viewing gallery above the control room in the centre of the incubator hall.

"It's the first 3 years of your life, condensed into a few minutes," Cole explained. "We wouldn't want you to feel you've missed out on anything."

# 64

The gallery reminded Cillian of a planetarium – a large curved screen with a bank of reclining seats in the middle. He sat a little apart from Cole and Gabrielle, then braced himself as the video started.

*Phase 1: Ectogenesis.* Music pulsed. A dot of light glowed on-screen. At first Cillian wasn't sure what he was seeing, but as the dot grew larger he realized it was a tiny embryo, just days old. It floated serenely in the darkness, then microscopic needles loomed into shot and began manipulating it, transplanting cells, injecting hormones and marker genes.

Coils of beautifully wound DNA twirled in a dance as hundreds of different sections were extracted, moved and replaced.

A string of coding ran across the bottom of the screen like an electronic ticker: GATC AGTC CGAT TGCA CATG. It looked like an abstract pattern, but Cillian knew that was his *own* DNA he was watching.

As the embryo grew, it was placed in an artificial womb, floating in synthetic amniotic fluid that glowed a soothing blue. Rotating images showed different enhancement techniques at each stage of development: genetic splicing, chromosome replacement, enzyme treatment, stem cell therapy.

At 39 weeks, valves opened, the fluid was drained and the baby was plucked from its glass womb, ushering in:

*Phase 2: Infancy.* A hard cut and Cillian saw himself in a prototype incubator, tended by an early generation RoboNurse; then as a toddler crawling around the glass nursery, playing with brightly coloured toys, oblivious to the antennae emerging from his sleepsuit.

Cillian glanced at Gabrielle. She was enthralled. "Look, here comes your first word."

He watched himself burbling contentedly, and somewhere in the sing-song jumble was "Dada".

"But where was he?" Cillian asked pointedly.

Gabrielle waved her hand in irritation to pause the film. "Who?"

"Dada. Where was he?"

"You didn't need him at this stage."

"Did he know what you were doing?"

"The one thing your father wanted was that you would never suffer the way his wife had suffered."

"So you turned me into a ... mutant?"

"That's not a word we ever use," Cole corrected.

"But it's the truth. The obsession with numbers and patterns, the weird time-shifting—"

"You've already felt that?" A frown creased Gabrielle's forehead. "How long has it been going on?"

"Since the Metro crash."

"Interesting." Gabrielle turned to Cole. "Make a note

of that. We'll need to filter out any instability with the next generation."

Cole tapped away on a tablet. For a moment Cillian felt like he didn't even exist.

When Gabrielle turned back, she caught his eye and sensed his discomfort. "There's nothing mystical about time shift," she explained. "The way animals experience time is connected with the speed of their metabolism. A fly races through life in a few weeks, processing information 7 times faster than humans. To a fly, the world unfolds in slow motion, which is why it's so bloody hard to swat them. When the world slows down for *you*, it's because your metabolic rate is speeding up. The trick is to control *when* that happens."

"With practice, you should be able to do it at will," Cole added.

Gabrielle stretched out her arm and put a hand on Cillian's temple. "The mind is so much more powerful than you can imagine. It's breathtaking."

# 65

Tess thrashed and struggled as she was lowered into the huge tank of dark liquid, but her limbs were held in rigid manacles, and no matter how hard she fought it made no difference.

As her feet were pulled into the viscous fluid she braced herself for the shock of cold, but strangely it didn't come. The liquid matched her body temperature exactly.

Deeper the manacles pulled her, immersing her legs, stomach, torso … as if they were going to drown her.

Paige had to turn away from the control room window. It was too much like watching someone being tortured.

"If we're going to prevent more terror attacks, we have to open up the girl's mind. Find all her secrets. We don't have a choice." It sounded so clean and clinical the way Gabrielle had described it, but she wasn't here now to see the reality of Immersive Drug Therapy.

"OK, she's in position," the operator said calmly.

Paige studied the monitors. Tess's body was now completely submerged in the liquid, with only her face breaking the surface.

"Inject the hormones," Paige instructed, anxious to get this over with.

If she stayed calm, she could breathe: that was the only way. As Tess stopped struggling, the ripples subsided and the liquid settled in a neat oval around her face. She remained absolutely still for a few moments, trying to regain her composure.

She was in a large, surgically clean room, flooded with diffuse light. Except for a narrow walkway around the edge, the entire space was taken up with the immersion tank. To the right was a long strip of reflecting glass. Whoever was doing this to her would be hiding behind that.

Lights started flickering on the domed ceiling; slowly they pulled into focus and coalesced into a billowing cloudscape, continuously moving, infinitely varied.

Needles emerged from the steel cuffs and a sharp scratch in her wrists punctured the tranquility. Tess tried to pull away, but as the drugs pumped into her veins she found it impossible to keep fighting.

At first there was just a tingling sensation, like mild electric currents swirling around the tank, caressing her skin, making it feel alive. Then as the seconds passed Tess started to lose all sense of her own body, as if the liquid was seeping into her flesh, dissolving the inhibitors in her brain.

The blossoming cloudscape became hypnotic. She knew she should close her eyes, try to resist, but the images were so soothing she couldn't bear to shut them out.

And as she let herself get absorbed into the space, Tess felt the doors in her mind swing open...

Memories started to spill out...

Long-forgotten images, trivial details loaded with emotion ... the sweet, comforting smell of her pillow ... a favourite pair of red shoes ... a robin sitting on the branch of a tree ... the sound of her mother's laughter; and each memory was brilliantly vivid. It was like randomly sampling her life, with every moment distilled to its essence.

Tess tried to take control, tried to focus on a single thought, but the flow had become unstoppable. It was like a flood of images bursting its banks, and as the walls that partitioned one memory from the next were washed away, all sense of privacy and identity started to break down.

Desperately Tess tried to protect the obscure corners of her mind, guard the quiet places where she hid her most personal moments, but it was no use. It felt as if she was drowning from the inside, and the only way to avoid suffocation was to let her memories out...

To talk.

At first it sounded like jumbled nonsense, meaningless words whispered at random.

"Send the feed upstairs, as well as to the recorders," Paige told the operator as she put on some headphones to listen.

Gradually Tess's whispering became more articulate: moments from favourite movies ... snatches of conversation with friends ... fragments of a pop song; then plunging deeper to memories of tastes and scents ... secret words ... traces of pure happiness and escape ...

... until finally the things Tess kept most tightly locked

away started to spill out: training drills, numerical codes, passwords, names of people, places, targets.

"It's all pretty mixed up," the operator said cautiously. "Let's hope the pattern recognition software can make sense of it."

Paige listened intently to the soft current of words, trying to find some coherence ... and then she heard, "*Derespino.*"

It was just a whisper, but it made Paige's blood run cold. She pulled off her headphones and gazed through the control room window. This girl must have been caught up in those clinical trials. And now she'd returned. Like a vengeful ghost.

"When will it stop?"

The operator shrugged. "We were told to extract everything."

"But you must know how long it takes. From previous subjects."

The operator hesitated. "We've only ever searched for specific information before. We've never tried to empty an entire mind. But it can't last long."

Paige heard the ominous tone in the operator's voice. "Why not?"

"The more barriers you dissolve, the greater the risk of psychosis. After a few hours of this ..." he glanced at Tess's floating body... "there won't be much of her mind left."

## 66

"This is the simplest demonstration," Gabrielle said, ushering Cillian into a test rig. "Doesn't involve any mental triggering. All you have to do is sit back and relax."

As the chair folded around him, it reminded Cillian of going to the dentist, only this chair had 2 high-tech box-arms that swung into position on either side. Cole guided his right forearm into one of the extensions and secured it with metal clamps that were padded with soft leather, then sprayed his skin with a cold blue gel.

"Anaesthetic," he replied to Cillian's questioning look.

"Doesn't sound very reassuring."

"A precaution, that's all."

There was a soft whirring as titanium plungers emerged from the sides of the box and pressed onto Cillian's forearm from opposite directions.

"We're going to try and break your arm," Gabrielle said calmly.

"No!" He tried to pull free.

"Don't worry. We won't succeed."

"I don't want—"

"Cillian!" Gabrielle raised a finger to her lips. "Don't make such a fuss."

Cole swung the opposite box extension into view. A thick wooden strut and a heavy steel bar had been clamped inside it, just like Cillian's arm.

"I'm not going to hurt you." Gabrielle touched the control panel and the hydraulics sighed into action. "I just want to show you how well you've been made."

Immediately Cillian felt the plungers push into his forearm.

"Your arm, the wood and the steel are all being put under the same pressure," Cole said, watching the force readings.

Cillian's eyes darted to the wooden beam, which was starting to bend, then back to his own arm. Already the flesh was distorting and swelling from the force of the clamps.

As he heard the hydraulics gear up to the next level he felt an intense pressure. It wasn't pain, but it was really uncomfortable.

Suddenly a horrible splintering sound cracked across the lab. Cillian flinched, but incredibly his arm was still intact. It was the wooden strut that had snapped into jagged pieces.

"This is when the tough get going." Gabrielle smiled.

A dull ache throbbed deep in Cillian's bones. He looked at the steel bar as it started to twist out of shape ... then at the force meters on the control panel, the numbers changing up so fast it was hard to read ... then at his arm which was finally starting to bend out of shape.

"STOP!" He struggled to pull his arm from the rig.

"Nearly there," Gabrielle said.

A horrible metallic groan echoed around the room as the steel bar buckled, then snapped clean in two, and *still* the pressure gauge was spiralling upwards.

"I think maybe that really is enough." Gabrielle leant across and touched the control panel.

With a sigh the plungers relaxed their grip and withdrew into the sides of the rig.

"Shit..." Cillian whispered, panting, staring at his arm as if it was something alien.

# 67

"It may seem hard to believe, but it's really just physics," Gabrielle said as she led Cillian deeper into the lab. "We've taken everything there is to know about materials science and applied it to genetics."

"It's why you've never had a broken bone in your entire life," Cole added with pride.

Cillian nodded cautiously; only now did it occur to him how odd it was that he was never ill. He'd always thought it was just luck.

"And it's not only your skeleton that's enhanced, but your muscles and ligaments as well. That's why you can leverage such strength." Gabrielle pointed to one of the RoboNurses parked in the corner. "You want to try that?"

"And do what?"

"Lift it up, of course."

"That's crazy."

"There's no room for small-mindedness in P8."

Cillian heard the flash of irritation in her voice.

"Unless you try, how will you ever know?"

"You could easily do it," Cole said smoothing over the awkwardness.

Cillian walked over to the RoboNurse and ran his hands over the solid casing. It was a formidable piece of machinery, with a massive counterweighted plinth to make the whole arm stable. "I don't think so."

"When you were fighting for your life, you didn't think," Gabrielle said. "Your body *reacted* to threat. Your survival instinct was the trigger."

Cillian's mind flashed back over the last week, remembering the incredible power that had surged through his veins as he rescued his father from the Metro, then fought with the intruder. "I can't really get angry with a nurse, though."

"Now you need to move to the next level. Because it doesn't have to be about emotions. Really it's about letting go of your boundaries," Gabrielle explained. "The human mind can be its own worst enemy, putting limits on what it can do."

Cillian looked at his own arms. Hadn't he just seen the incredible strength of his bones? Even so, lifting several tons of metal...

"You know what the strongest biological material on Earth is?" Gabrielle said, second guessing him again. "Limpet teeth. Ridiculous." She laughed. "But if nature can gift a mollusc clinging to a rock, why can't we do it for you?"

Cillian closed his eyes and let his mind plunge inwards, trying to read the mathematics of his own body, translating biochemistry into numbers...

For a skeleton to be stronger than steel the fundamental building blocks would have to be reinvented, the chemical bonds realigned. But mathematically, theoretically ... it was possible.

*He* was possible.

Cillian clamped his arms around the RoboNurse and tightened his grip until the metal pressed hard into his chest.

This *was* possible.

Numbers don't lie.

His body tensed with effort and suddenly energy surged through him. He leant back, taking the weight into his arms ... slowly the RoboNurse eased away from the ground, exposing a loom of control cables disappearing into the floor like dangling roots.

Cillian breathed deeply, relishing the heaviness.

3 seconds...

4 seconds...

He relaxed again, letting all the energy drain into some unknown reservoir, and the robotic arm dropped to the floor.

Gabrielle and Cole gave him a small round of applause.

Cillian gazed at the vanquished RoboNurse. "All this time ... and I never knew."

"It just shows how safe your life has been," Gabrielle observed. "Until a few days ago, survival had never been an issue."

Suddenly Cillian's mind filled with a yearning for new sensations. "What else can I do?"

"Addictive, isn't it?"

"How far have you pushed this?"

"*How much further is there to go?* That's what you should be asking. That's when it gets really interesting."

"So why the secrecy?" Cillian asked. "Think of the benefits all this could bring."

"Sometimes the truth makes people feel ... uncomfortable." Gabrielle chose her words carefully. "There are things we can't say or do in Foundation City with all its civil liberties and advisory councils. Biological Development isn't a smooth process, we've had our setbacks. Not everyone turns out as well as you."

It jolted Cillian back to the real world. "Gilgamesh."

"There you go."

Dark memories of the mutated, imprisoned children flooded back to Cillian, and he felt an angry stab of guilt for allowing himself to be caught up in Gabrielle's vision.

"Where's Tess?"

"That chapter of your life is closed—"

"What have you done with her?" Cillian demanded.

"She's telling us what she knows. That's all."

"Let me talk to her."

"Really, I don't think that's such a good idea."

"I don't care what you think. I want to see her."

Gabrielle hated it when experiments started talking back. But looking into his determined eyes, she realized that she would have to indulge Cillian.

For now.

# 68

When would it end?

When could she close her eyes, give up the fight?

And just let go.

Tess could hear a voice talking...

Her own voice.

Murmuring endlessly.

For hours.

Or was it minutes?

She was too exhausted to know.

Too exhausted to concentrate.

Too disorientated.

But the voice wouldn't stop.

On and on.

Letting everything out into the world, spilling herself.

Yet it didn't *feel* like her voice.

The real her was still in hiding.

She'd retreated deep inside to make a last stand.

Holed up like a lone gunman.

A sniper, picking off her enemies.

But there were so many of them.

Closing in from all sides.

So many.

Destroying everything in their path.

Dismantling her mind, wall by wall.

Soon there would be nowhere left to hide.

She'd fought so hard, but it was useless.

And now all her demons crawled out of the rubble to torment her...

The dead.

In the hot, smoking gloom of the tunnel.

The dead.

She knew they were here.

Waiting for her...

A photograph fluttered in the darkness. She reached out...

Caught it.

A family snap – Cillian and his father, blowing out birthday candles.

Tess felt herself smile.

Until dark spots of blood seeped across the picture, staining the happiness red.

More photographs, falling like snow.

Thick snow.

Thousands of family moments...

But all of them bloodied.

Dark red blood crawling across memories like a cancer.

Blood that *she* had spilled.

Run.

Get away.

A dot of light up ahead...

Refuge.

If she could get to the light, she would be safe.

Salvation.

But as she ran, a cold hand grabbed her ankle—

She tumbled.

Desperately reaching out to break her fall...

Nothing there.

Nothing to grab on to.

She plummeted in the darkness.

Down into an abyss.

An endless nothing.

*CRACK! CRACK!*

Gunshots echoing off hard walls.

She was facing Cillian, her trembling fingers gripping the Luger, holding it to his head.

*Trying to destroy what should never have been created.*

But he wasn't frightened, his too-perfect face was smiling.

"It's all right, Tess."

So calm.

"Do what you have to."

*CRACK! CRACK!*

And it wasn't him any more.

It was Blackwood.

Reaching out to help her.

To guide her.

To comfort her.

She touched her finger to his head—

*CRACK!*

And a neat bullet wound appeared.

"It's all right, Tess."

He slumped to his knees, into a pool of his own blood...

So much blood.

A lake of blood surging through the tunnels, washing away walls and platforms and train tracks.

Tess slipped as her feet were swept from under her.

She was lost again.

Adrift on a sea of blood.

And guilt...

Blood and guilt.

*CRACK! CRACK!*

2 more bullets...

She was standing in front of a mirror on Judgement Day.

But there were no bright lights, no Pearly Gates.

This was the bathroom in the Bullet Train.

Speeding her to damnation.

*"How to get the most refreshing and hygienic afterlife—"*

Tess hit *Mute.*

She stared into the mirror, watching herself age ... her skin wrinkle ... her hair thin and grey ... her eyes dull; she felt her body ache with fatigue...

A body that was as wasted as her own life.

A life of misguided choices.

Of misery and murder.

Her sense of failure was so overwhelming, it begged only one question...

When—

Would—

It—

End?

# 69

"What have you done to her?" Cillian stared through the glass at Tess's body floating in the dark liquid like a corpse.

"Don't feel sorry for her," Gabrielle said calmly. "She is ignorance and death."

"*What have you done?*"

"We're doing what the police can't." Gabrielle was unwavering. "It's been days since the Metro attack and they've got nowhere. But in a few hours..." She glanced at Tess. "We know she's Revelation. She may even have planted the bomb that killed your father. So don't feel sorry for her."

Cillian felt his anger melt into confusion.

He stared through the observation window. "*That was a tragedy. It should never have happened.*" Tess had said that to him only yesterday. If she really believed that, how could she have actually planted the bomb?

And if she *was* a murderer, why wasn't he lying dead

in the crypt of the cathedral? So many things refused to fall into a pattern.

"She's probably been with them since she was a child." Gabrielle scanned the preliminary pattern-recognition results. "Indoctrinated. Trained to kill."

Suddenly Tess's body started to spasm, sending ripples across the tank. Paige and the other operators hurriedly checked their monitoring screens.

"It's just her nerves reacting," Gabrielle said. "Always looks worse than it is."

But Cillian couldn't watch any more. "Whatever she's done, it doesn't justify torture."

"I think you're wrong there. She's a dangerous extremist. And she's waged war on everything Foundation City stands for."

"I don't want to be part of this."


Gabrielle found him sitting on the floor in the corridor outside. "It's a lot to take in, I know."

"Just leave me." Cillian refused to look at her.

"You have to get some perspective on this." She sat down next to him. "For 3 billion years, life has been driven by random mutations. But because of what we're doing here, we can *choose* who we are ... *what* we are. Some people can't handle that, which is why they've turned to violence to destroy our work." Gently she put her hand on Cillian's shoulder. "To destroy creations like you."

"But when *you* destroy people, that's OK." He glared at her.

"In a thousand years time, people will look back and be grateful for the courage we showed. For not flinching. The truth isn't always comfortable, but that doesn't stop it being true."

"Everyone thinks they're driven by truth."

"Revelation is full of yesterday's people. All their ignorance achieves is pain and suffering. Science is the only way we'll survive. And that *is* the truth." Gabrielle stood up, straightened her clothes and walked away.

For a few minutes, Cillian didn't move. He no longer knew where he could go, or where he belonged.

The control room doors clicked open and a young woman came out. She glanced at him uncomfortably and went to speak, then thought better of it, turned and hurried away.

Cillian watched her go, waiting to see if she would change her mind. "The only mistake she made was to follow, to do as she was told."

Paige stopped in her tracks.

"There were people who controlled her. Made her think it was her duty to obey. I'm sure you know what that feels like."

Paige turned and looked at him. He could see the guilt in her eyes.

"But in the end, she made her own choice." Cillian stood up and walked towards Paige. "Isn't that what counts? Making a choice?"

"It's too late now."

"Don't say that."

"She's finished."

"I've seen Tess fight. She doesn't give up that easily."

# 70

The sound of her own breathing.
    The feeling of her lungs expanding and contracting.
    Slow and steady.
    There was nothing else.
    No liquid engulfing her.
    No images bombarding her mind.
    No memories tormenting her.
    Now there was just emptiness.
    Stillness.
    Peace.
    Perfect peace stretching in all directions.

"Tess ... Tess..."
    The voice was faint, calling out from far away.
    Faint, but familiar.
    "Tess... Open your eyes."
    *Leave me.*
    "Tess." The voice was impatient. "Come on!"

Why did he want to pull her away from the tranquillity?

What difference did anything make now? She had nothing left.

She was lost.

Fingers touched her eyelids and gently lifted them.

Tess winced. The light was dazzling, painful.

"We haven't got long," a different voice urged. A woman's.

Tess felt arms around her, lifting her up, carrying her, wrapping her in warm clothes.

She could smell his skin, and it was so familiar.

She opened her eyes. Her face was resting on his shoulder. She watched the muscles in his neck tense as he carried her...

Running down dimly-lit corridors lined with pipes.

Following the woman—

Who swiped open all the doors—

Who knew all the security codes.


The bitterly cold air hit Tess like a shockwave. Immediately she started shivering.

"Stand up."

Hands placed her feet on the ground, but her legs buckled and she slumped.

2 arms caught her. Held her tight.

"Stand up! You have to stand."

Willpower.

She concentrated on tensing her muscles.

Taking her weight until she was standing.

Swaying unsteadily, as her body's memories started to trickle back.

"Look at me."

Slowly she opened her eyes ... pulling him into focus...

"Cillian," she whispered.

"You have to run."

She shook her head.

"You *have* to."

"Not on my own. Come with me."

"I'll only put you in more danger. It's me they really want."

Tess saw the woman behind him, standing by the service doors. "Cillian – let her go," she urged. "Now!"

He gripped Tess's shoulders, trying to will her to her senses. "Remember your training. It'll come back to you. But you have to run. These people will kill you."

Tess looked down. "I deserve it…"

"Don't ever say that!" His warm hands cradled her face.

"I'm sorry," she whispered. "For everything."

"I know."

Tess looked into his perfectly identical eyes.

After everything she'd done…

After all the reasons there were to hate her…

He didn't.

"Can you forgive me?"

"Doing the right thing in a screwed up world … that's the hardest thing of all."

Gently Cillian leant forward and kissed her.

Briefly.

Softly.

"Now run. And don't look back. Ever."

# 71

Run. Easier said than done.

Before she could run, Tess had to walk.

Block after block, trying to get her body and mind working again.

Trying to rebuild the mental landscape that had been obliterated in the immersion tank.

As she wandered from quarter to quarter in the bitterly cold small hours, her eyes hunted for the familiar: buildings, shops, streets, anything that would give her a jolt of recognition.

But it was a strange time of night. This was when the City healed itself; when garbage was spirited away and power cycles switched to recharge; when burnt-out bulbs were replaced and faltering traffic signals repaired; when an army of nocturnal cleaners removed the dust from millions of desks.

She tried to think of people she knew, friends in the rolling-estates who could shelter her. But as her mind picked its way through the list she realized the chilling truth: *everyone* she knew was linked in some way to Revelation.

Tess huddled tight against the biting cold wind. Her only chance of survival was to get out of Foundation City altogether.

Far away.

She was running from Revelation and she was running from P8. If she could escape into the wilderness of the Provinces, maybe she would finally be beyond everyone's reach.

But with no identity card, no money, no smartCell, it would be almost impossible to move.

Almost.

She would need to draw on every drop of training she once had—

If only she could remember it.

Think.

Concentrate.

Head down, hands driven into pockets, Tess walked, marshalling her thoughts, step by step.

Training drills.

Survival techniques.

They were all in her mind...

Somewhere.

# 72

"After all the intelligence we've gifted you, how could you let yourself be manipulated by her?" Gabrielle couldn't comprehend his logic.

"I wasn't manipulated," Cillian insisted. "I showed compassion, pity – human emotions. Things you haven't got around to correcting yet."

"So you *chose* to help a terrorist? And that's better?"

Suddenly the door opened and Cole entered. "Paige has gone as well. It was her codes that unlocked the service areas."

"*Shit!*" Gabrielle hurled her smartCell to the desk in frustration, sending pencils skittering to the floor. "I *knew* Paige was weak. I should've done something."

"Security are on it," Cole said hurriedly. "We'll bring her in."

"*Both* of them. I want them both back here in 24 hours. Back here ... or dealt with."

"OK. It's done." Cole hurried away.

"You see?" Gabrielle turned back to Cillian. "It won't do any good. It was a futile gesture. Tess will pay for what she's done, one way or another."

"Do you really believe she had any more choice than those victims in your glass cells?"

"Spare me the moralizing. She murdered your father."

"But she saved me."

"Only so she could *use* you."

"And you haven't? All I've ever been to you is an experiment. But when Blackwood's finger was on the trigger, you were nowhere to be seen. Left to you, I'd be dead."

"So I played brinkmanship with your life. And? Children have to learn about risk the hard way."

"From the woman who's spied on me my whole life—"

"Observed."

"Just like you *observe* those children being tortured in Gilgamesh."

"Tortured? You really think that's what we're doing?"

Cillian was incredulous. "You don't see what's wrong? Do you?"

"Our patients are cared for with every possible medical intervention—"

"You've *engineered* children. To experiment on."

"To ensure the survival of many more. Nature's been doing it for billions of years. It's called evolution. The difference is, nature generates mutations then lets them suffer and die. It's pitiless. We create with meaning and purpose. We nurture."

"You exploit. For profit."

"Don't be blinded by sentimentality, Cillian."

"What about compassion?"

"What use would a surgeon be if she was too afraid to cut open a living person? You want to put an end to suffering, you need clear thinking. Real courage is following logic to the end point."

"You call Tess the extremist … you should listen to yourself."

"Well I certainly can't listen to you any more, not until you've calmed down." Gabrielle turned and headed for the door. "I hope you're not going to be one of those experiments that ends in failure, Cillian. I really thought you were better than that."

# 73

*06.00 – Continental Trading Time.*

Tess waited for the first wave of the rush hour to make her move; it was slower going but there were more places to hide in a crowd, and staying anonymous was her only chance of getting through the Central Transport Axis and out of the City.

With no money the Metro wasn't an option, so she'd been forced to use the Moving Walkways that threaded through the Downtown Quarter. Originally built for people with health conditions and mobility impairments, the Walkies had long since been taken over by those who found that walking interfered with their ability to surf the Ultranet.

Tess's eyes scanned the crowd, searching the faces for anyone who was alert to their surroundings rather than glued to a screen ... someone who was hunting.

How many would they send?

Where would they attempt the hit?

The Walkie came into the CTA by Platform 12, but the Bullet Trains Tess needed left from 74–101. It meant she'd have to work her way along the entire length of the concourse, past all the shops and cinemas, risking the myriad CCTV cameras with their facial-recognition software.

Suddenly Tess felt scared. She'd never make it through this. P8 would almost certainly have tapped into the City Cockpit and they'd corner her.

She crouched down by a metal balustrade and closed her eyes, huddling her arms tightly around her body.

What was the point of running, anyway? Escape to where? To oblivion? Everything she knew was in Foundation City, and now she was exiling herself—

*Don't think like that.*

Don't worry about the future. Just focus on the next few hours.

Keep going; keep pushing.

Tess forced herself to stand up and look out across the vast concourse. She'd been trained to get through places like this. She'd done it before; she could do it now.

The Urban Jungle, that was her best chance. A tropical rainforest built *inside* the CTA, sustained by a complex array of jets and humidity sensors. She could use the cover of the trees to avoid the surveillance systems.

But as she approached, and the first steam cloud of the microclimate engulfed her, Tess's paranoia ratcheted up. Wouldn't the dark places in the rainforest give cover to her enemies as well?

She veered away and hurried up the escalators to Level 1, where express food outlets lined the gallery. Immediately Tess felt more anonymous in the frantic push of people grabbing breakfast between train and office.

She walked briskly, crossing continents in a few strides: bagels and bacon, churros and hot chocolate, steamed rice and kimchi.

Near the higher platform numbers the food outlets became family-friendly diners for groups catching the Bullet Trains and shuttles to the International Airport. In this melee Tess saw her chance.

She picked up a free magazine and sat near a young mother with a small mountain of luggage, who was trying to wrangle 2 energetic toddlers. They all had ski jackets – obviously heading to some snow resorts – and crucially both the kids had large strawberry milkshakes in front of them.

Tess flicked through the magazine, waiting for the inevitable.

*"For God's sake, Lucy!"*

A bright pink slick sped across the table and cascaded onto the mother's jeans.

"Why can't you be more careful?" The mother leapt up, but it was too late.

Lucy thought it was hilarious, which provoked her younger brother to start splashing his hands in the milkshake.

"No! Enough!" The mother yanked her kids away from the table. "NO!"

Their laughter suddenly morphed into tears.

Tess grabbed a bunch of tissues. "Here, let me help." She leant over and started mopping up the pink goo.

"Thank you." The mother sighed.

"It's always the most disgusting drinks they spill," Tess said brightly as she tried to contain the slick.

"We're going to smell of bloody strawberries the

whole trip." The mother looked at the lurid stain on her jeans and her 2 pink-spattered kids. "I've got to clean this off."

"I think there's a washroom over there." Tess pointed across the walkway.

"Are you in a rush?" the mother asked hopefully.

"I am really..." Tess glanced at the departures board.

"If you could just watch our cases, I promise I'll be quick." She looked at Tess with pleading eyes. "Just for a second? Please?"

"OK. Sure."

"Thank you *so* much. Really, I'll be quick." And she dragged her screaming kids towards the toilets.

The instant they were out of sight, Tess dumped the tissues and picked up the smallest case, hurriedly unzipping the outer pockets and rifling through them.

Second pocket in, she got lucky: tickets, passports, even some spare cash. She took the adult ticket and a small amount of cash, tucked everything else neatly back in place, then hurried away from the diner.

Tess headed straight for the Bullet Train. It was still 20 minutes before departure, but she hoped that by leaving the other 2 tickets the mother wouldn't realize she'd been robbed. Even so, it would be a long 20 minutes waiting for the Bullet to pull out.

Tess found the carriage and scanned the ticket across the Virtual Conductor panel.

The doors didn't open.

She tried again.

*"Please scan the other 2 in your party,"* the Virtual Conductor politely instructed.

"Shit." Tess searched the panel for other options, then touched *Meeting on Train*.

*"The other members of your party are minors,"* the train responded.

"I know that," Tess muttered impatiently, and touched *Meeting on Train* again.

*"No record of your party on the train."*

"Shit, shit, shit!"

*"Have you become separated from the minors in your group?"*

"Just stop being so bloody helpful and let me in!"

*"Do you want assistance?"*

"When did it get so hard to get on a train?" a man's voice chuckled.

Tess turned round and saw a smiling young ski-bum waiting behind her.

"Do you mind?" he waved his ticket.

Tess stepped aside, the ski-bum scanned his ticket and the train doors sighed open for him.

Now. Go for it.

Tess barged in after the ski-bum, but the doors were too quick and slammed shut, trapping her.

Immediately an alarm started to sound.

*"Please stand clear of the doors. Please stand clear of the doors."*

Desperately Tess tried to lever the doors open, but they were too strong and pain was searing into her arm. She jerked backwards and just managed to pull herself free.

But the alarm didn't stop.

*"Assistance is coming. Assistance is coming."*

A ticket inspector was making his way down the platform towards the flashing light above the forced door.

Tess turned and ran—

But seconds later she saw 2 strangers closing in on

her from opposite directions: a man in a business suit and a woman in jogging pants, urgently pushing through the crowd.

They were talking to each other on smartCells.

And they had her locked in their sights.

# 74

"Move! Move!"

No longer time for any niceties.

Tess pushed and barged and elbowed her way through the crowd towards the nearest exit.

Just get outside. She'd have more options in the street—

When suddenly a man loomed into the station through the huge revolving doors. He looked normal enough, jeans and a thick leather jacket, but he immediately locked eyes with Tess.

She spun back around and bolted for the escalators, hoping to disappear in the chaos of the food level.

As she ran past the diner she saw the mother and her 2 young kids, their clothes blobbed with dark stains where they'd washed off the strawberry milkshake. The mother was frantically searching through the zip pockets of their luggage, looking for her missing ticket. For a fleeting moment she glanced up and saw Tess bolting through the crowds.

Too late to apologize now.

Tess saw a service door and tried to barge it open, but it was locked; even garbage removal needed a swipe card.

She veered into a latte bar, leapt over the counter, scattering cakes, pushing baristas out of the way, spilling jugs of foaming milk, then crashed through the store room out into a service corridor.

Running hard through stripped concrete and white-washed walls, the smell of disinfectant mingling with the trash.

There must be another way out of the CTA.

There *must* be.

Back down the corridor she heard crash-doors echo. P8 weren't giving up.

She remembered her training and stopped dead – in the worst crisis, block out the world, find a moment of calm to think.

Tess closed her eyes and listened...

Hostile footsteps hurtling towards her.

Under that the deep rumble of trains departing.

The murmur of the commuter crowd.

And something else ... in the background...

Water.

Running water.

Tess snapped open her eyes and zeroed in on the sound. A large blue downpipe, too wide to wrap her arms around, punched through the floor and stretched up to the roof.

Rainwater harvesting.

Every new building had to have a harvesting system to cope with the extreme summer droughts.

It was her last hope.

Tess ran along the service corridor to the next

emergency exit and kicked it open. Immediately a siren started to whine, but she was way beyond caring about alarms now.

Scrambling breathlessly up fire-escape ladders, she emerged onto the roof gantries – and was stunned to see torrents of water cascading down the skin of the domes. She crouched down and stretched out her fingers. The glass was warm; the entire surface of the dome was heated. Snow was falling heavily, but the instant it touched the glass it melted and was channelled away through large gullies running under the walkways.

Tess followed the gullies as they converged on a grating-covered manhole where the water thundered down into a sinkhole.

She leapt from the gantry and plunged her hands into the icy water to haul the massive grating up, desperately trying to ignore the freezing pain that cut into her fingers.

Tess pulled harder, her hands numb, her mind screaming at her to let go, but she refused to listen; she just kept pulling.

And suddenly the grating swung back.

She peered down into the blackness. It was like the most extreme water flume, too steep and too bitterly cold, but it was her only hope.

Tess closed her eyes, clamped her arms around her head, and dropped—

Slamming into the sides of the pipe.

Gulping in mouthfuls of air.

Choking on the water.

A moment of terrifying free fall as the pipe spat her out into a massive underground chamber...

And she plunged into a deep, dark pool of icy blackness.

Tess clawed her way to the surface and gasped in lungfuls of damp air, every fibre in her body trembling with the cold.

Treading water, she span around to get her bearings. The walls were dotted with service lights. She was in a cavernous underground reservoir directly under the station; this was where the rainwater was stored and recycled, but if she didn't get out of the cold, it would also be her tomb.

There was a large outlet in one of the walls with metal rungs leading up to it. Stencilled onto the wall was a single word: *Overflow*.

Overflow would lead to storm drains.

Storm drains fed back down to the river.

The river meant freedom.

Tess lunged forwards and swam towards the metal rungs, each agonizing pull with her arms drawing her a few metres closer.

20 metres.

15—

Something brushed against her legs.

She screamed and kicked out violently.

The thing backed off.

Tess peered down into the gloomy water. A shadow fluttered past her legs, swimming fast, circling her.

What the hell was down there?

She thrashed in the water, trying to get away, but the thing wouldn't give up.

A tentacle stroked across her body, then snapped tightly round her leg.

"NO!"

She reached down, fingers frantically trying to prise the thing off.

It was metal.

A cold metal snake-arm.

And with one powerful yank it dragged Tess under water.

# 75

Gabrielle found him at the top of the building, gazing out of the panoramic windows at the fury of the rush hour below.

"Cillian?"

No response.

"What we're doing here ... it matters." Gabrielle was trying hard to be patient. She had to keep reminding herself that moods and emotions needed to be wrangled until they could be strained out of the genome. "What can I do to help you understand?"

"I understand just fine." Cillian turned to look at her. "Whatever gifts I have, those children in Gilgamesh are paying the price."

"You want to talk about childhoods? Fine. Let me tell you about mine." Gabrielle perched herself on the ledge. "The years spent in hospitals, blighted by illness. Lying in my bedroom listening to the other kids playing outside. Longing to put sickness behind me, to feel well without worrying how many months remission would last. Being too frightened to think about what I wanted to do when I grew up, because I didn't know if I would grow up."

Cillian could see the pain of those memories in Gabrielle's eyes.

"If there is a God, then he cursed me. Medical science was the only thing fighting my corner. When they finally cured me, the doctors told me to pick up my life and carry on. But by then the whole world had fallen ill: climate change, pandemics, drug resistance, pollution sickness. How could I live if the world was dying?" Gabrielle looked out across the atrium. "*This* was the answer. Change what we are. Make us strong enough to survive. Is that too much to ask?"

"It's wrong to build people in a test tube," Cillian said. "It shouldn't be done."

"You make it sound so cold. But I built it from *me,* Cillian. I harvested the eggs from my own body. I screened and selected the fathers; I created 123 embryos. Each one enhanced and nurtured, each one with its own unique gifts. I gave them everything and right now they're scattered across the City, living their lives anonymously, finding their niche, unaware that they are a brilliant new generation."

A feeling of disgust rose in Cillian's guts. He remembered finding a spider's nest in the palm tree on his balcony when he was a kid, peeling back the tight knot of leaves to see *hundreds* of tiny spiders packed into a writhing mass, scurrying over each other. There was something obscene about one spider spawning so many offspring...

And Gabrielle was no different.

She was too greedy for life.

# 76

Tess lunged to the surface and managed to snatch precious gulps of air before being dragged back under. Desperately she tried to tear herself free, but the metal tentacle refused to loosen its grip.

Even though the bitterly cold meltwater stung her eyes, Tess could see that the thing attacking her had 8 tentacles attached to a black metal body. It was like some weird mechanical squid. And she wasn't its only catch. A dead pigeon was coiled in another snake-arm, while 2 nets protruding on stalks had snared a pulp of leaves and drowned plastic bags.

Suddenly Tess realized what this thing was: a Disposal-Bot. Flotillas of them patrolled the sewers 24/7, and one of them must have been deployed here to scoop up any debris that got washed down from the domes.

For a brief moment she felt relief...

Until she heard the thumping sound of blades chopping the water. She looked up. The bot was dragging her towards a processing unit in the far wall where she would be shredded and filtered, just like all the other unwanted trash.

She lashed out wildly, struggling to free herself, but that just provoked the bot even more and a second arm whipped out and coiled around her torso.

The more Tess fought, the faster she burnt through the oxygen in her lungs, the harder the cold ate into her muscles, the tighter the snake-arms gripped...

It was no use; the Disposal-Bot was just too strong.

She could never win.

After all her defiance and rebellion, she was finally going to be killed by a dumb, dutiful robot.

Tess stopped struggling, relaxed her limbs and surrendered.

In the calm of her final moments, she thought about Cillian...

How he had come back for her when he should have abandoned her; how he was the only person left who believed in her.

A flash of guilt jolted Tess to her senses. She owed it to Cillian to keep fighting. She *wasn't* going to be killed by a dumb, dutiful robot.

She was better than that.

The chopping suddenly got louder. More blades powered up, as the processing unit prepared to be fed.

Seconds. That was all she had left.

Moving smoothly to avoid further inciting the bot, Tess wrapped her arms around its body. Her searching fingers ran over its surface and found glass spheres dotted along the circumference.

Sensors.

Sonar? Infrared?

Perhaps she could blind it. She hammered her fist into one of the spheres, trying to smash it.

The glass was too tough.

Gripping the bot tightly, she jerked her body to one side, hoping to drag them both off course, away from the chopping blades.

But the giros refused to be thrown.

She saw clouds of bubbles rising from the salivating shredder's vents—

Her fingers brushed against a gnarled ring on the bot's body – some kind of access port.

Tess gripped it and twisted.

It wouldn't budge.

She twisted harder ... fingers numb, the last spoonfuls of air draining from her lungs ... harder—

Suddenly the cap loosened and flew off in her hand.

Water gushed into the machine, fusing circuit boards, shorting power supplies, drowning it from the inside.

Snake-arms twitched frantically in a last defiant attempt to live, then the Disposal-Bot went limp and spiralled down into the darkness of the giant tank, tentacles flailing uselessly behind it.

Tess burst to the surface, gasping in the air. Utterly exhausted, she swam to the metal rungs, hauled herself up the wall and rolled into the overflow tunnel.

She lay there for a few moments, lungs heaving, body shivering. She so wanted to close her eyes and rest, just for a few minutes...

*No.*

That's how hypothermia got you.

Tess forced herself onto her knees. She had to get away, had to get warm again.

Stumbling, crawling, she made her way towards the

circle of light at the end of the tunnel ... and emerged into a wall of one of the service canals that criss-crossed the City. 3 fully loaded TrashBarges were lined up, waiting to join a convoy that would head downriver and out to the BoilDowns.

Tess pulled back into the shadows and let the first 2 barges pass, then she leapt ... landing with a heavy thump near the stern of the final barge.

Quickly she rolled under a tarpaulin that covered the trash, and stripped off her soaking-wet clothes. She clamped her arms around her body and rubbed her flesh, trying to get some feeling back. At least under the tarpaulin there was some respite from the weather.

Trembling, exhausted, alone, Tess crouched in the darkness, not daring to think about what would happen next.

All she knew was that she was still alive.

She had not given up.

# 77

"Maybe we haven't told him enough," Gabrielle reflected as she watched Cillian on the CCTV monitors, pacing back and forth in front of the panoramic windows. "Maybe if he understood where he really fitted in, we could capture his imagination."

"He can't handle what he's already been told," Cole said pointedly.

"Because it doesn't quite make sense. You know how his mind's been designed. He needs to see *everything* to understand the particular. Compulsive pattern recognition."

"It's too big a risk. I don't think he's ready."

"His father could never let go," Gabrielle continued. "Interesting how we've magnified stubbornness as a collateral effect."

"What if you show him everything and he hates it? What happens if he gets angry? You've seen how he reacts under pressure."

"It won't be a problem."

"How can you be so sure?"

"Because at the end of the day, he's just an experiment," Gabrielle said calmly. "*My* experiment."

# 78

The hot pipes running through the TrashBarge hold were lifesavers. Sprouting from vats that digested bulk food waste and turned it into biofuel, the pipes made perfect drying rails and it wasn't long before Tess could get into warm clothes again.

She poked around the hold: old computers and robotic components, smartCells and magazines, shoes and synthetics, TVs and tyres, power cells and plastics in every colour imaginable.

So much waste.

And this was just one barge. At least 100 convoys left the City every day; Foundation was like a giant monster excreting high-tech and synthetic debris.

Tess knew she had to make a move before the Trash-Barge reached a BoilDown, or she'd be arrested for trespass. In police custody it would be too easy for P8 to find her.

Cautiously she lifted the edge of the tarpaulin. She

was at the back of the boat, and this was the last barge in the convoy. A couple of kilometres further down the Great Canal she could make out the next convoy, and beyond that the City skyline disappearing into the mist.

She clambered onto the deck and looked around. There were running boards on either side, leading forwards to the bridge cabin. That's where the crew would be.

Should she take the fight to them? Or should she play dumb? If she concocted some story about running away from home, maybe they would turn a blind eye to regulations and help her.

Maybe.

Taking no chances, she hunted around for something to use as a weapon and managed to yank a metal bar off a bedstead. She tested its weight, wielding it first as a club, then a spear. It would have to do.

Slowly Tess crept down the running board, braced for the slightest sign of the crew.

Closer ... and closer...

If they were paying attention, they should have seen her by now.

She reached the back wall of the cabin, slowly edged forward, looked inside ... and smiled. The cabin was empty: the captain was a computer.

Tess swung open the door and stepped out of the biting wind. Banks of digital panels lined the cabin walls, controlling everything from satellite guidance systems to the burn-rate of the biofuel generators.

A beautiful old wooden stool sat in front of the monitoring panels – perhaps when the TrashBarge docked a pilot took over – but the long trek out to the Provinces had been delegated entirely to computers.

Ignoring her pangs of hunger, Tess perched on the seat. An electronic chart slowly unfurled across the main screen as the TrashBarge made its way down the Great Canal; the convoy's route was going to take it across a daisy chain of vast lakes. Tess vaguely remembered from her history lessons that these had once been picturesque rural towns and valleys, all flooded to create the reservoirs that let Foundation City drink and wash.

In the far distance was the ridge of mountains that she had last seen from the speeding Bullet Train. Beyond those mountains lay her only hope. She needed to find a small community where she could start again.

It wouldn't be easy. A stranger arriving from the City would arouse suspicion. Her best bet would be to lie low for a while until the news moved on.

Tess gazed up at the mountain ridge. There must be caves up there, somewhere she could shelter, make a fire, hunt small animals, live off the land for a few weeks. It was the best her exhausted mind could come up with; at least now she had a plan.

She checked the charts to find the closest point between the Great Canal and the mountains. There was still time to close her eyes and grab some sleep...

But unlike Tess, the computer-driven TrashBarge never closed its eyes, never rested.

As she'd climbed out of the hold, the onboard sensors had detected a tiny change in weight distribution. And inanimate loads shouldn't move.

A systems alert was activated, and the TrashBarge's CCTV powered up to take a look. Someone, somewhere watched as a teenage girl made herself comfortable in the cabin. An unauthorized presence on the bridge breached shipping regulations. It would have to be investigated and dealt with.

Traces. There were always traces.

# 79

The elevator reached the bottom floor, but didn't stop. It kept going down to levels unmarked on the indicator panel.

"Not many people are allowed this far," Gabrielle said calmly.

Cillian didn't feel reassured.

"One of the things I love about science is its humility," she said. "I have no illusions about myself. I'm just a link in the chain. We all are, and anyone who thinks differently is deluded."

The elevator finally eased to a standstill but the doors stayed shut. The control panel demanded fingerprint verification. Gabrielle touched her thumb on the screen and only then did the doors open, flooding the elevator with light.

They emerged into an expansive hallowed space, silent and calm. In the very centre of the glossy marble floor were 2 highly polished titanium statues, life-size depictions of a strange creature. One posed standing up, the other crouched on all fours like a hunter.

Cillian gazed at the statues, struggling to make sense of what he was seeing. It was confusing; the creature was a disturbing amalgam of the familiar and the strange...

Then suddenly it pulled into focus.

"My God..." he whispered.

"Not quite. But I think He would've approved." Gabrielle walked towards the statues. "This is the real goal of our research, Cillian." She reached out and gently touched the gleaming metal surface. "Human perfection."

The creature had a muscular torso rippled with an exoskeleton, 4 limbs that were a strange fusion of arms and legs, a face that was human but with individual elements rearranged and supplemented.

"Meet H+," Gabrielle said. "She's the future. The epitome of intellect and athleticism. As comfortable on 2 legs as 4, pre-adapted to survive the environmental changes that are now unstoppable and the social chaos that will follow."

She paced around the statues, proudly pointing out various innovations. "Gills that work alongside lungs – for a world that's flooded. Skin that photosynthesizes sunlight into energy – to survive famine. Eyes that work across a broad range of frequencies – to see toxic radiation. Limbs that can regenerate, an immune system resistant to nearly all known diseases ... this is the ultimate human being. And you, and me, and all those children in Gilgamesh ... we're just stepping stones on the journey to *this*."

For a few moments Cillian was dazzled by the beauty of the creature, built with such searing logic. "It's incredible," he whispered.

"She is," Gabrielle said with quiet pride. "I knew you'd understand."

"But..."

Gabrielle turned her piercing gaze on Cillian.

"What about everyone else?"

"What about them?" Gabrielle seemed puzzled.

"If this is 'Human Plus', where does that leave humans? Ordinary humans, who are alive today?"

"I'm not interested in ordinary."

"There's a world full of people who need genetic cures and vaccines—"

"Am I my brother's keeper?" Gabrielle said sharply.

"You can't just write off 10 billion people."

"People who did *nothing* as the climate changed, despite all the warnings. People who ignore warnings reap the whirlwind."

"So this is some kind of revenge?"

"No. It's just the inevitable. Evolution is brilliant but cruel: it punishes weakness and stupidity."

"What kind of justice is that?"

"Justice has nothing to do with it. If natural selection was fair, life on Earth would've been snuffed out as soon as it began. That's just a simple fact. But now humans can define what we are." She rested her hand on H+. "And this is it."

"No. It isn't." Cillian stared at the gleaming, arrogant statues. "This isn't what it means to be human at all. This is just about survival."

"What else is there?"

"*Everything*. Everything that makes life worth living."

"Oh, you mean love and art and all those fuzzy ways of thinking?" Gabrielle smiled. "We tried so hard to design sentimentality out of you, Cillian. Love is just an illusion, a trick to remix the genes with every generation. And music and literature and culture, they service the remix.

They're the veneer that masks what's actually going on."

Cillian finally saw just how pitiless she was. "I want nothing to do with this. Or with you."

"I understand. It's strong stuff, isn't it? That's why we need to make some adjustments."

Cillian felt suddenly uneasy as Gabrielle walked towards him.

"You haven't turned out quite how we'd hoped."

"I don't want adjusting." He backed away. "I just want to leave here. Now."

"OK. That's fine. If that's what you want, you can go."

Why was she being so understanding?

"Let's at least part on good terms." Gabrielle opened her arms as if to give him a final hug, but Cillian shook his head. "After what you've done?"

He turned and strode towards the elevator doors.

Moments later he heard her footsteps behind him. Cillian spun around defensively, but Gabrielle just smiled. "You'll need me to unlock the doors."

Innocently she lifted her right hand to show her thumb, and in that moment of distraction she struck—

Her left hand lashed out, gripping Cillian's neck.

He felt a sharp pinprick in his flesh.

"I'm so sorry."

Immediately weakness started flooding into him.

He tried to pull away, but she held his neck tightly. "I'm not going to hurt you," she spoke softly. "I just want to put you back into development."

"No!"

"You won't remember any of this. Not even as a bad dream. And you'll wake up so much better."

Fight.

Before it's too late.

He tried to gather his energy, to slip out of time, but the toxins flooding his body were confusing his reactions.

He was *not* going to end up back in Gilgamesh.

They were *not* going to wipe him clean like some malfunctioning machine.

"NO!" Exploding with rage he smashed Gabrielle's arms aside. As she stumbled backwards he saw a half-discharged microsyringe in her hand.

"What's in it?" Cillian swayed uneasily. "Tell me!"

He lunged towards her, trying to grab the syringe, but Gabrielle dodged backwards and ran towards the elevator.

Without thinking, Cillian leapt, but now he was off balance, his senses confused.

He smashed into her too heavily, slamming her to the floor.

She gasped with pain. With shock.

Fighting to co-ordinate his movements, Cillian dragged himself to his knees and rolled Gabrielle over. Blood was oozing across her shirt.

The syringe had punctured her heart.

She gasped, but it was barely audible.

Already the colour was draining from her face; her lips were tinged with grey.

"You should've let me go!" Cillian said. "Why didn't you let me go?"

Gabrielle mustered all her energy, fighting the drugs that were shutting her systems down. "You ... can never be out..."

She coughed, tried to speak again, but it was incoherent.

A last groan...

Then she fell silent.

Cillian stared at her, but she didn't move again. Her body didn't even twitch.

He dropped to his knees, slumped over her, trying to wrestle back control.

She was a predator.

Trying to kill him.

He'd defended himself.

There was no choice: one of them had to die.

Cillian touched his neck. The weakness had stopped spreading; his body was containing the chemical.

Escape. He had to escape or it would all have been in vain.

His eyes darted across the walls, hunting for CCTV, but there was nothing. Perhaps the secret inside this room was so sacrosanct it had to remain invisible.

His mind flashed back, piecing together the fragments of the building he'd seen over the last 2 days, constructing a map.

*I see it.*

Struggling to contain his remorse, Cillian bent down, grabbed Gabrielle and dragged her body across the room, leaving a bloody wet smear on the smooth marble. At the elevator he yanked her hands up and touched her thumbs on the control panel...

*Identity Confirmed.*

The doors opened.

He dropped Gabrielle's body, but as she fell, Cillian heard her smartCell clatter to the floor. He picked it up. A whole string of message updates from P8 Security scrolled across the screen.

They had a trace on Tess.

She was trying to escape along the Great Canal.

And they were closing in fast.

# 80

Tess couldn't help smiling. No matter how smart the world got, water still flowed downhill. Right now that gave her the perfect chance to get away.

Several kilometres back, the convoy had started to break up, as individual TrashBarges peeled off for different destinations. Her barge was heading for one of the Highland BoilDowns, which meant it had to navigate a series of 40 canal locks that climbed into the mountain foothills.

Fully-automated and computer-controlled, these locks bore only a passing resemblance to the hand-cranked wood and iron gates from centuries ago. Now huge synthetic shutters rose and fell on hydraulic rails in a continuous, noisy techno-dance. It was ugly and soulless, but it didn't matter as no-one was out here to see. One feature had survived brutal modernization: the towpaths, and as the barge rose through the first lock, Tess leapt onto dry land and ran.

She picked a line straight across the heathland and headed for the saw-toothed mountain ridge.

Even though the low shrubs had caught the most recent snowfall, stopping the ground underneath from freezing hard, it was still tough going. Every intake of cold air stabbed her lungs, and her muscles craved energy, reminding her how little she'd eaten in the last 24 hours.

It was only willpower that kept Tess going.

After half-an-hour of pain her body settled into a rhythm, her breathing steadied and her legs found a fluid momentum.

Now running on autopilot, she could finally think...

To the west, a massive bank of black clouds was edging closer: snow. She needed to find shelter before that came or she'd be in deep trouble. Yet for all the menace in the clouds, Tess felt a strange sense of peace.

As she ran on, she knew that she had never been so vulnerable. If she twisted her ankle, or didn't find food, she would die out here. And yet the dangers were no match for the exhilarating sense of freedom.

All her life with Revelation she had lived in fear – fear of the unknown, fear of change, of the future – and everything she'd done had been an attempt to escape from that fear. But now, faced with the total indifference of this raw landscape, Tess realized that she could never escape it. Fear was all around her, waiting for her at every turn. But if she looked hard enough into its dark heart, she could still find freedom.

An hour later, she came to a frozen stream. She stamped her feet on the glistening ice until it cracked, then hacked out a hole and scooped handfuls of water into her dry mouth. It was so cold and clean, it seemed to rush into every last cell of her body.

She stood up and looked at the mountain range stretching into the distance. *This* was where she belonged. It felt so right—

Until 4 dots moving on the horizon jolted her heart.

Please ... no.

She stared at the dots, willing them to be nothing more than wild animals.

But they were too organized and too relentless.

They were men.

Moving steadily towards her, never breaking formation, closing with deadly intent.

They could only be assassins. P8 or Revelation? It made no difference now.

Tess screamed with frustration. She'd dropped off the networks; she'd left no trace. How the hell had they found her?

She glanced up at the approaching dots. Why wouldn't they just let her vanish? She was no threat to them out here. She would never be a threat to them again.

But killers didn't listen to reason.

She would just have to keep running.

Tess turned, leapt across the frozen stream and bolted.

She would not let them catch her.

She would not.

# 81

Cillian strode down the boulevard listening to the emergency sirens screaming in the distance. Police and fire vehicles thundered towards the plumes of smoke belching from the Downtown skyscraper.

It was just as Tess had said at Gilgamesh: P8's security was built for intruders, not traitors. Which had made it easy for Cillian to wreak havoc...

As soon as the elevator was above ground level, he had activated the emergency stop, then scrambled through an escape hatch in the ceiling, emerging into the central core of the building where massive electricity cables ran alongside giant pipes that fed the genetic labs.

Now Cillian knew what he was capable of, everything seemed effortless. He ripped the pipes from the wall, splitting them in 2 with his bare hands, releasing the volatile chemicals. Then he shorted the power cables and outran the ballooning explosion that followed.

Once fire was raging in the heart of the building, the

security doors automatically unlocked and he was away.

Cillian didn't glance back at the plumes of acrid smoke. All his focus was on freedom. But as he walked, he realized that everything seemed different now. It was as if he'd been reborn inside P8, and he felt a confidence, an invincibility, that he'd never known before.

Others seemed to sense it too. Instinctively pedestrians moved out of the way as he walked, glancing warily as if he was a surge of disruptive energy.

He checked Gabrielle's smartCell. More security updates pinged onto the screen. Oblivious to the fire now tearing through their headquarters, the assassins were closing in on Tess. They'd been offered helicopter support but had turned it down. They knew their target was heading for the mountains which meant the only way to flush her out was the old-fashioned way: on foot.

It meant Cillian still had time.

# 82

The victim chose himself.

Cillian had been waiting by the traffic signals for less than a minute when he saw the modish man on a motorbike pull up. It was a steel blue Benedetta Overdrive, and it was clearly the man's pride and joy, as he couldn't resist glancing in the mall windows to catch his reflection astride the sleek, powerful machine.

Probably some fashion vlogger who got kickbacks for promoting the next big thing to a million followers, Cillian mused. And now he was flaunting his success by showing the world that he could afford to ride a gas-guzzling Overdrive because the super-tax was small change.

Yes, this one deserved to lose his motorbike.

Cillian waited until the signals were just about to change. He watched the vlogger click into first ... eyes focussed on the red light ... hand revving the throttle ... enjoying the distinctive engine sound...

And Cillian made his move.

*Impossibly fast.*

In a split second he was standing in the middle of the road.

"What the hell—?"

Cillian plucked the vlogger from the motorbike and slammed him onto the tarmac.

Before the Overdrive could even start to topple, Cillian caught it, roared the engine and climbed on, as he spun it in the opposite direction.

"NO!"

Cillian looked over his shoulder to see the vlogger scrambling to his feet. "It's *mine*!"

"Take the Metro," Cillian said. "Save the planet." Then he opened the throttle and sped away, leaving the vlogger with nothing but the distinctive engine roar of the Benedetta Overdrive ringing in his ears.

The highways were mainly used by hauliers, and the snowploughs kept them clear 24/7 because it was trucks that kept the Provinces alive, delivering everything that couldn't be downloaded.

Right now though there wasn't a truck in sight, which meant Cillian had the Spine Road to himself.

He scrolled through the menus on the Overdrive's dashboard, selecting everything that would make his life easier: vehicle-tracking *Off*, auto-gear change *On*, gyro-stabilization *Active*.

Then he crouched low over the fuel tank, opened up the throttle and relished the incredible sense of speed, as he rode towards the mountains.

# 83

In the wide open snowfield, Tess was easy prey and she knew it.

No matter how many times she changed tack, the 4 black dots doggedly followed, until finally at her wits' end, she slumped to her knees. Running wasn't going to work. They were never going to let her go.

She had only one chance left: take the fight *to* them. The saw-toothed ridge was really close now. That would be her battleground. She'd lure them in and fight on her own terms.

Which meant she needed a gun.

Tess's eyes scanned the horizon...

A few kilometres back she'd crossed a lonely set of tyre tracks heading east. She'd been running too hard to care where they led, but now she realized they may be the quickest way to a weapon.

She set off around the base of the ridge at a steady pace, and after a quarter of an hour intercepted the tracks again, followed them through a narrow gulley and emerged to see 3 tractors working their way slowly up and down the mountain foothills. It couldn't be a farm – the landscape was too hostile and the only buildings were a few temporary cabins clinging to the hillside.

As she got closer Tess saw that they were planting trees, hundreds of trees in neat, straight lines, probably to satisfy some international carbon quota.

She couldn't see any people. All the hard work was being done by the satellite-controlled tractors. The lead one was patiently drilling holes, the second plucked saplings from a crib and drove them into the ground, while the third tractor towed a machine which packed each hole with compost and fertilizer.

A 4x4 was parked outside one of the cabins, inside which the technicians were keeping warm, and beyond that were various storage units.

Hugging the landscape, Tess looped around to stay out of the line of sight, then dropped down and snuck into the largest storage cabin.

Any space that wasn't taken up with tractor spares was given over to huge pallets of food and crates of beer. It looked like the crew was going to be on the hillside for a while.

Tess stuffed her pockets with energy bars, then rummaged deeper into the supplies, prising open lockers, until she found the weapons rack: a couple of shotguns and 3 sniper rifles. Not the most obvious tools for planting trees, but essential for anyone working this far out. She knew that there had been a return of scavenging wolf packs from the north, and in a remote place like the mountains you could find yourself in real trouble.

She tried each weapon in turn. As she slid the bolts

and checked the sights Tess could feel her training clicking back into place. Finally she settled on a Koch sniper rifle, but just as she was loading her pockets with ammo the door behind her swung open—

"You came a bloody long way to steal a gun."

Tess spun round and saw a man with close-cropped hair and a weathered face staring at her. She swung the rifle up to prevent him stepping any closer, but the man just shrugged. "Come on ... you haven't even had a chance to load it."

Tess held her aim, braced for the man to attack.

"What the hell are you doing out here, anyway?"

"Don't even ask." She edged back, trying to give herself time to load the magazine.

"Perhaps I should raise the alarm, then."

"I really wouldn't do that," Tess warned.

"There are 3 of us in the cabin—"

"By the time they come, you'll be dead."

The crop-haired man held her gaze. "Look, what kind of trouble are you in?"

Tess froze; she'd been fighting the world for so long, she wasn't sure how to react to a few kind words. She looked the man up and down. He reminded her of one of the farmers from her old village. He'd probably got this job because he knew the land as only someone who's grown up on it can.

"Some men are hunting me," Tess replied.

"How many?"

"4. They're going to kill me."

Crop-Hair nodded thoughtfully. "What have you done?"

"It's a long story."

"But who's in the right?"

Images flashed across Tess's mind: the carnage of the Metro bomb, the horrors of Gilgamesh, Blackwood's bloody corpse lying in the cathedral crypt, the cruelty of P8.

"I don't even know how to answer that any more," she said quietly.

"Well ... do you deserve to die?"

Tess shook her head.

"Look, I've got a radio—"

"That won't help."

"We could call the police."

"It's beyond the police."

The man pointed at the rifle in her hands. "You really think you can stop these men with that?"

"I can try. If I get up to the ridge, find a place to ambush them. Take them out one at a time."

"I've heard worse plans." Crop-Hair nodded. "But if I let you go, how do I know you won't just kill me as well?"

"You don't. But I won't."

Neither moved a muscle. Tess and the man just stared at each other. Then slowly a grin crept across his face. "That's not such a bad answer."

And he stepped aside, clearing the way to the door. "Make sure you take plenty of ammo."

Tess grabbed 2 more boxes off the shelf and stuffed them in her pocket.

Keeping her eyes locked on Crop-Hair, braced for any twitch of muscle that would signal an attack, she made her way to the door. But the man just stood there with his hands in his pockets.

"Good luck," he said as she stepped outside into the cold wind.

# 84

Getting unexpected help from the total stranger lifted Tess's spirits.

With the Koch rifle slung across her back, she scrambled up the rocks into the belly of the saw-toothed ridge. A few minutes into the climb she stumbled on the remnants of an ancient track worn into the granite.

Perfect.

She bolted along the path, putting real distance behind her, zigzagging higher and higher—

*CRACK!*

An echoing gunshot pulled her up sharply. Tess span around, hoisted herself onto a narrow ledge and peered down...

The 4 assassins were fanned out across the encampment, guns trained on Crop-Hair and his co-workers, who were slumped on their knees, hands behind their heads. Further down the hill the tractors carried on diligently planting trees, oblivious to the danger.

Tess could hear the killers shouting at their hostages, demanding answers, but getting nothing. Furiously one of them lashed out, kicking Crop-Hair in the face, sending a spray of blood across the snow.

Enough.

Tess plucked the Koch from her back and trained it on the clearing. The autofocus sights locked onto each of the assassins in turn: 2 men, 2 women.

The older woman unholstered her pistol and strode menacingly towards Crop-Hair. She asked him something, he shrugged. She yelled at him, but still he said nothing. Brutally she jammed her pistol into Crop-Hair's face and started counting down.

Tess breathed slowly and half-squeezed the trigger. Data illuminated the rifle sights: distance, wind speed, trajectory correction.

She designated the assassin's head as the target.

And fired.

The sound of the rifle shot cracked across the landscape, the assassin's head jerked with the impact and she toppled backwards, falling like a tree into the snow.

Immediately Tess tried to pick off another one, but the killers were already running for cover.

Crop-Hair and his colleagues seized the moment of chaos, scrambled to their feet and dashed to the 4x4. They clambered inside, gunned the engine and skidded away down the hillside.

The camp was tranquil again.

Nothing moved except the industrious tractors.

Tess swept her rifle left and right, searching through the sights, but the assassins were well-hidden. Right now they'd be scouring the side of the ridge with infrared binoculars, looking for any trace of her. She knew the smart thing was to keep moving, but she also knew she'd never get a better chance to kill them than this.

So she hung on, waiting for them to move, willing them to reposition. If they wanted to hunt her into the ridge they'd have to cross a small strip of open ground; all Tess had to do was stay calm and fast, then she could pick them off.

A flurry of movement as one of the assassins bolted from behind a storage cabin. Tess panned the rifle, trying to hold him steady in her sights, as he dodged from side to side—

But the range data refused to settle.

No time to wait—

Override the numbers—

*Crack! Crack! Crack!*

Shots peppered the ground just behind the killer.

Tess adjusted.

*Crack!*

The target stumbled, gripping his leg in agony.

Tess lined the sights up on his chest to put him down for good—

When suddenly stone splintered all around her, as bullets ricocheted off the rocks. Tess recoiled, swinging back behind a boulder as another hail of bullets shattered home.

The running assassin had just been bait to make her reveal her position and she'd fallen for it.

Quickly Tess crawled away from the boulder, slithering on her belly until she was back on the path and could run higher.

Following the track was risky. It was the most obvious route, but now survival was about speed; she had to get away from her last position as fast as possible.

As the path veered left on the final ascent to the ridge, Tess glanced down again at the tree plantation. There was a trail of blood in the snow from the assassin she'd wounded. He was dragging himself by his hands, trying to get back to the cover of the cabins. She could hear his cries of pain, calling out to the others, begging them to help, but they refused to break cover and put themselves in the line of sniper fire.

Suddenly the wounded man's screams became more panicked as he realized that he was now lying *directly* in the path of the planting tractors, which were doggedly pressing on with their daily quota.

Frantically he screamed out, begging for help, but still the other gunmen ignored him.

And the tractors were stopping for no-one...

The first one bumped slightly as the front tyres crunched over the man's body, mangling his hips, then a terrifying howl rang out as the drill bored down through his torso.

Tess couldn't watch any more. She turned away, but she'd paused for a moment too long—

Shots rang out, high velocity rounds impacting the rocks around her, showering the air with lethal stone shards.

Searing pain cut into her head.

Tess slumped back, cradling her face in her hands. She could feel blood pouring from the lacerations. Her eyes were burning and her vision was clouded by a chaos of swirling reds and blacks.

She tried to open her eyelids, but every blink was agony, like dragging sandpaper across her eyeballs.

Eyes clamped shut, she groped her way back from the edge, crawling on hands and knees until she could feel the smoother rock of the path.

Her hands searched the boulders until she found a pocket of snow. Grabbing as much as she could, Tess held the snow to her face and let it melt against the warmth of her skin, trying to wash the stone splinters from her eyes.

She looked up, willed herself to focus.

But it was useless.

Her vision was gone. She could barely see the path, let alone defend herself.

# 85

Climbing blind was madness, but Tess didn't have a choice. The assassins would have seen she was injured and be hard on her heels.

So she staggered on, arms outstretched, trying to avoid stumbling and falling off the mountainside. But she knew this couldn't end well.

She paused for a moment and stilled her breath, allowing her hearing to find clues in the air...

Crows circling overhead.

Wind across the ridge.

In the far distance an engine revving. Had Crop-Hair managed to raise the alarm? Was help coming?

The clink of rocks below, steady and relentless. The 2 remaining assassins were coming for her.

Tess clambered on, desperately trying to think of a survival plan, when just for a moment her footsteps made a strange echo. She clicked her fingers. It sounded as if there was a hollow close by.

Quickly she ran her hands across the rocks until she found a gap just wide enough for her body. She stuck her head through and whistled softly. It was some kind of small cave.

This was good. This could work.

Tess slipped into the hollow and slumped against the rock on the far side. From this position she could hear the assassins approaching, she would see their shadows crossing the entrance. All she had to do was set the Koch to burst fire and aim at the light.

Easy.

Unless she killed herself with the ricochets.

And provided both assassins were close together.

And that they didn't toss a grenade in here first.

Still, no plan was perfect.

As Tess waited for the end, her fingers explored the ancient rocks. A trickle of damp had become home to some moss, and the floor was pitted with small indentations where water dripping for thousands of years had worn the granite away.

Higher up the wall her fingers found some regular patterns carved into the rock. She squinted in the darkness, peering really close, and could just make out a line of ancient symbols.

Who had left their mark here? A Neolithic worshipper? Someone hiding from predators? What would it be like to talk to that ancient race now, to try to explain how everything had changed, and yet in some ways nothing had changed? Despite all the high-tech in the world, people were still hunted down, still forced to run for their lives.

An angry burst of bullets in the gulley outside shattered her train of thought.

She braced herself, finger on trigger.

When strangely, *return* fire rattled around the rocks.

*2* different weapons. A firefight.

That didn't make sense. Why would the assassins be firing at each other?

Tess strained her ears, trying to piece together what was happening from the jumble of violent sounds.

She heard shouting, some kind of warning, then another burst of shots and a woman screamed in pain. She was hit. Badly.

More footsteps, moving really fast and close, scurrying across the rocks above her, fast as a lizard, but much heavier.

Tess gripped her rifle, aiming it at the cave entrance, focussing everything on the blurry patch of light. As soon as a shadow appeared she would shoot. That was the only way to stay alive.

No time to find out who was out there.

No time to ask questions.

Just shoot and survive.

Gunfire ignited again. Closer this time. Another weapon fired back.

Tess concentrated on the echoes. Both gunmen were moving, but one was much faster than the other.

Moving and firing.

Really fast.

*Impossibly* fast.

Suddenly the shooting stopped. There was a strangled cry, then a terrified scream.

Silence again.

Footsteps approaching.

But that couldn't be right. *4* assassins. She'd killed 1. The tractor had impaled a second. She'd heard 2 die up here.

*So who was still out there?*

Tess held her breath, finger poised on the trigger.

The footsteps crunched closer on the loose rock outside.

She braced herself for the kill...

And then someone spoke. "Tess."

A shadow moved across the entrance to the cave.

"Tess... "

She had to shoot, do it now or die—

But she knew that voice, even though it wasn't possible. "Cillian?"

"It's all right. They won't harm you now."

Tess staggered to her feet and stretched out her arms, reaching towards the blurred shadow. She put her hands up to Cillian's face and touched his skin.

"You found me," she whispered, fighting back tears. "You found me..."

She felt his face move under her fingers as he smiled.

"I did owe you," he said.

He put his arms around her and they held each other tightly.

# 86

P8 had contingencies: if attacked, they were to retreat to designated secure precincts far below street level.

The fires had barely been extinguished and the rubble was still smouldering when P8 started ramping up standby systems, transferring all their work to the new labs.

Everyone in the organization worked fast, as many of the running experiments were time-critical and if they weren't back online quickly, years of research would be wasted.

But Cole's job was different. He had a Priority One assignment. Gabrielle had set out a detailed protocol to be followed in the event of her death, and that took precedence over everything else. She and Cole had even rehearsed the routine when Gabrielle was still alive, so he knew exactly what to do.

Immediately after he'd found her body crumpled on the floor, Cole activated the Regeneration Notice. Minutes later fluids were being pumped through Gabrielle's corpse, circulating oxygen, nutrients and plasma, trying to hold off death's decay.

Now as Cole followed the gurney down narrow corridors, he looked pensively at the bottles of vital fluids clamped to the stretcher and the technicians hurrying alongside, diligently checking monitoring screens. It was odd to see so many people making such a fuss over a corpse.

The gurney stopped by a high-security entrance; Cole swiped his card across the reader, touched his thumb on the pads and the doors opened.

Inside was a row of massive glass incubators bristling with oxygen feeds, IV drips and drug-lines. Each cradle was tended by 3 complex robotic arms, controlled by banks of computers in a dedicated SmartTech nursing station.

Cole watched as the technicians gently loaded Gabrielle's body into an incubator and started the lengthy process of plugging her up. He turned to the head nurse sitting behind an array of control panels. "What are her chances?"

The nurse studied the screens. "The toxins caused multiple organ failure, there are early signs of necrosis, her heart was punctured causing a severe internal haemorrhage ... it's going to make Regeneration complicated."

"Not the answer I wanted."

"It's the way things are, I'm afraid."

Cole gazed at Gabrielle's cooling body. "We *need* her. You do understand that?"

The nurse stopped tapping her keypad and glanced up from the screens. She couldn't remember the last time she'd see Cole so moved. "If it can be done, we'll do it," she said, trying to sound confident.

"Gabrielle's ideas built everything. All this…" There was a sense of wonder in Cole's voice. "If she's not with us for the next phase … there is *no* justice in the world. No justice."

"Death has always been a challenge," the nurse admitted. "But we're pushing back a little harder every time." She pointed to another incubator on the opposite side of the room. "We nearly succeeded there. But he was just too far gone."

Cole crossed the room and looked at the body in the incubator. It was split wide open so that robotic arms could carry out intricate micro-surgery, while nanobots nurtured the new organs being grown in situ from stem cells. Despite the traumatic procedures, the man's vital signs looked surprisingly stable. His face was even starting to lose the ghastly pallor of death.

Cole had only met Cillian's father on a few occasions, but it was enough to know that Paul would approve of how they'd tried to bring him back to life. What better way to defy the terrorists who had bombed the Metro than to cheat death?

"He looks pretty good to me," Cole observed.

"Don't be fooled. He'll never open his eyes again. He's brain-dead. The best we can do is keep his body ticking over."

"Well, I'm afraid …" Cole turned and slowly paced towards the Nurse, "… that won't be good enough for Gabrielle. She believed that with enough money and resolve, anything was possible." Cold determination tinged every word he spoke. "Now prove it."

Anxiously the nurse glanced back to her screens. "We'll try."

# 87

In the darkness, all Tess could feel was the biting wind on her face. For a few hours it was a relief to keep her eyes closed and block out the rest of the world.

They had made their way down from the ridge with Tess clinging to Cillian's back. At the plantation encampment he'd bathed and bandaged her eyes, delicately removing as many stone splinters as he could. It would have to do until they could get to safety and a hospital.

Now they were on the Benedetta Overdrive, speeding towards the coast and the promise of freedom on the Continent.

They rode deep into the night, not stopping until they arrived at a rocky headland overlooking a massive port blazing with lights. This was where the towering cruise ships docked to disgorge their passengers onto high-speed shuttles for Foundation City. It made the port useless for Cillian and Tess as it would be teeming with security systems that were almost certainly monitored by someone in P8's network of informants.

So they rode on, following the narrow roads that wound around coastal inlets, until eventually they came to a rundown harbour, the sort of place where fishing trawlers had been docking for centuries.

Quotas had wiped out the local fleets years ago, but it was impossible to stop small boats from slipping in and out of these obscure coves. The locals who ran them were already plugged into the black market to sell their catches, so Cillian hoped it wouldn't be too hard to find someone willing to trade the weapons they'd stolen. 4 rifles in return for safe passage across the sea – it was a bargain for someone.

A few hours later, Cillian and Tess were sitting on a quayside wall, listening to the soft lap of the dark water, waiting for a small boat to finish refuelling.

"Do you think we'll ever come back?"

Tess breathed in deeply, filling her lungs with the fresh, sharp air. "I don't see how we can."

"It doesn't feel right, though, running away."

"You're sure you want to go through with this?"

"We're out of options, aren't we?"

But Tess could hear the reticence in his voice.

"What about the terror attacks? What happens now Blackwood's dead?"

Tess thought for a moment. "There'll be a power struggle inside Revelation. The Suprema will be jockeying for position. I guess it depends who wins."

"So it could get even worse?"

"I hope not. For everyone's sake."

"And Generation Zero? Will they still be targets?"

"They'll always be targets." She moved her hand along

the wall so that it brushed against Cillian's. "That's why we have to get away. Find somewhere to hide."

Cillian put his hand over hers and held it tightly. He stared out across the ocean. At night it looked so sinister, black and huge and unforgiving, as if warning everyone that they ventured out on it at their peril. And yet the warmth Cillian and Tess drew from each other's hands made even that brooding ocean seem a little less daunting.

"I'm glad it's you, Tess."

She rested her head on his shoulder. "Me too."

"As long as we're together, we'll find a way. Somehow."

"Right! Let's get going," the fisherman called out, as he untied the mooring ropes.

Cillian turned round to take one final look at the country he was leaving. He could still see the faint glow of Foundation City's billion lights in the night sky. Despite everything, he felt a sharp stab of remorse as he remembered the violence of that final encounter with Gabrielle.

He didn't have a choice. He had to remember that.

She'd tried to kill him and he'd defended himself.

But...

There was something else that disturbed his mind. Something wasn't quite right ... something didn't fit the pattern...

He replayed the scene again, stepping through it slowly, focussing intently on each detail, each moment ... from different angles—

And his heart lurched.

*I see it.*

A disturbing image locked in his mind. There, behind Gabrielle's body, he could see a word carved in small letters on a limb of the polished titanium statue.

A single word: *Huxley.*

A name.

Not a serial number.

Not the Latin for a new species.

Not H+.

A name.

*A person's name.*

Cillian clicked through his memories until he was looking directly into the creature's face ... staring into those eyes...

And now he realized that this was no bland prototype; its expression was too troubled, too complex. It had the face of one who had already experienced hope and pain.

H+ wasn't just a statue...

She walked the Earth.

Living.

Breathing.

The new human.

Nausea overwhelmed Cillian as he finally understood.

"What is it?" Tess knew something was very wrong. "Cillian?"

But his mind was numb with shock.

Tess slipped the bandage from her eyes and managed to focus on his face. "What's happened?"

"It's too late," he whispered. "They've created her. It's too late."

Tess could feel fear radiating from his body like a primal force. "Let's just get to safety. Then we can figure out what to do," she urged.

"It's no use." Cillian shook his head. "Nowhere is safe now. We're history. Wherever we run, it won't be far enough."

Immediately, instinctively, Tess's training kicked in, pushing her to survive no matter what. "Listen to me." She reached out and held his face. "First we run. Then we get strong. Then we decide who to fight. Understand?"

Cillian thought how cold her fingers felt on his face.

*"Do you understand?"*

He looked at Tess searchingly. There was not a flicker of doubt in her scarred eyes.

There couldn't be.

Because doubt was weakness.

And they both knew that weakness would not survive.

Not in the future that was now coming.

A future where being human would not be enough.

# Acknowledgements

One of the great joys of writing is rewriting.

Going back to a manuscript, digging deeper, exploring new paths and discovering fresh vistas is a really fascinating journey.

Like any expedition, it's best done in good company, and I have been extremely fortunate to work with Walker Books. Denise Johnstone-Burt and Daisy Jellicoe have been a brilliant editorial team, combining encouragement, wisdom, criticism and patience in just the right proportions.

Huge thanks also to Hilary Delamere, Julia Kreitman and everyone at The Agency for all their support, advice and bold thinking over many years.

Living with a writer can't be easy, but I'm extremely grateful to Karen and Hugo for finding a way to do it, and for all their love and support along the way.

# "How long does it take to write a novel?"

Thanks to the software logs, I can now give an accurate answer...

Excluding all the reading and research (of which there was a lot!) *Maladapted* took 35,624 minutes to actually write. Which is 594 hours.

Looked at another way, that's 37 seconds for each and every word.

Not that I'm obsessed with numbers.

To find out more, visit www.richardkurti.com
Or take a look at Twitter @Richard_Kurti

And if you want to *see* what a writer gets up to, visit RichardKurtiWriter on Instagram

# Also by Richard Kurti

**Shortlisted for the UKLA Book Award**

**Longlisted for the Carnegie Medal**

"Strikingly original." Anthony Horowitz,
author of the Alex Rider series

"Ratchets up the suspense and dread with unrelenting
urgency, compelling readers to keep the pages turning."
*Kirkus Reviews*

"Readers who might be drawn to *Watership Down* but
prefer a faster pace will relish the antics of the monkey
tribes of Kolkata." *Guardian*

"Kurti ... creat[es] an animal world of utter credibility,
easily as subtle, complex and devious as our own."
*Irish Times*

"A powerful allegory in the style of *Watership Down* or
*Animal Farm*... Effective and unnerving."
*Publishers Weekly*